"He'll keep a ___ ___ ___ eep him in check. I've ___ ___ ___ many years."

I stood tall and proud, happy to finally be acknowledged by those assembled. I was ready to fulfill my purpose in life at last.

"How will Verwyn react, though?" The wizard who spoke was a lady with bushy, dark brown hair and oddly flat black eyes that seemed to absorb light. "He's already proven skittish, and he has no love of us or reason to trust this blue-haired child."

"We could play on his sympathies," another wizard, a tall man, mused. "Verwyn has, traditionally at least, been a caring and protective sort. It's part of his innate nature, written in his soul. He's someone who couldn't walk away from someone injured or in pain."

I looked at Lord Ceolwyn, confused, and saw the life drain from his expression. The color in his cheeks, the twinkle in his eyes, retreated in an instant.

The tall human began speaking again, but as I looked in his direction all I saw was a bow in his hand and an arrow ready to be nocked.

I started to back away, knowing immediately where this would end.

"That's right. Pretend to be running away from us."

"Stop!" Lord Ceolwyn put his hand on the tall wizard's arm, and for a moment I thought he had a better idea. That I would be saved from whatever pain the other wizard wanted to put me through. But I was wrong. "He's in my care. Ysili is my ward. I'll do this myself."

That's when I ran.

Still Waters
and Other Tales

Tam Chronin

Cover designed by Joshua Stomberg

This book is a work of fiction. Names, characters, places, and incidents either are products of the author's imagination or are used fictitiously. Any resemblance to actual persons, living or dead, events, or locales is entirely coincidental.

Tam Chronin
Visit my website at www.tamchronin.com

Independently published

Table of Contents

We Are as Dreams

Mother."

Nalia hears the thought and turns her attention to it, knowing that the word is said to her, about her.

"Child," she replies in her thoughts, then, immediately, she smiles. "Esier, my daughter."

They silently agree upon a spot, a mountain overlook, and the time of year is spring. Flowers enshroud the lands below. It's a cacophony of color, and each bud radiates the delicious magic of things to be.

The landscape brings them both pleasure. The two goddesses share that for a time in silence, just to share a moment in time.

But there is purpose in their meeting, and it is not just idle sharing of the beauty of nature upon this day.

"I want to warn you about Agruet," Esier says when she's had her fill. "He's hiding something."

"He hides everything," Nalia says, patient and amused as a mother often is. "I know he sets your nerves at edge. It's only natural that the two of you would make each other uneasy. Knowledge is your sphere. Secrets are his. It's fine, daughter. Everything is as it needs to be."

Everything is as it needs to be.

The words were meant to be a placation, but Nalia feels an uneasy twist within her greater awareness that the words mean more than she knows. Esier nods, knowing this, but they have no more need of words between them on this matter.

"Mother."

The word summons Nalia from a matter of interest, and she turns her attention to the source with irritation.

Agruet.

The name is like an epithet these days. From the very beginning he has questioned all things.

Now he is back for more.

The lands around them are warm with summer and heavy with heat as they appear together. Insects buzz, and it makes Nalia's teeth clench as soon as she has them. "Listen to me! Mate with me!" they cry, drowning out everything else. She could silence them, but they're part of the system of things, and with their silence there would be other, more annoying things in their place.

"Here, of all places and times?" Nalia demands of her son. Exasperation is the mildest of emotions she holds for him at this moment.

"It's a beautiful, lazy day," Agruet replies with a placid smile. If there's any deeper meaning, or if there's not, he gives no hint by expression or overt thought.

From one trickster god to another, Nalia is convinced that every nuance is of note. Agruet means to have her irritated and on edge. What he means to say must be a sort of a trap.

"What do you think of the sentient beings we've created?"

It's such an odd question. "They're creatures. Creations. We've done an amazing job of it, haven't we? I'm particularly partial to the faeries. Aren't they adorable? Like flying flowers, with magic no other race can beat."

"You don't like the humans the most?" This time he gives overt emotion, surprise that must be feigned, put on as a deliberate act.

"Why would I?"

The teeth of Agruet's verbal trap snaps shut. "Because they're so talented when it comes to treachery." He laughs and laughs.

Instead of the reaction Agruet was looking for, Nalia grins. "One can admire and feel akin to a creation without having it be their favorite."

"One can." There's disappointment on his face, and this is also overly expressed. His reaction either meant he was surprised into showing truth, or this is just another act.

With him, one never knows.

"Mother?"

It's a plaintive cry that tugs on her thoughts, and Nalia appears without thought. "Yes, my son?"

The autumn air is filled with the scent of earth, of rot, of decay. Trees are shedding their brilliant leaves, blanketing the earth in scarlet and brown like blood and meat. This season, this reminder of impending death, never came when the world was young. When the world did not have Baedrogan in it.

His physical form towers over her, lean and lank. "It's been a while since we talked."

Of course it had. Nalia takes her son's hand and nods.

"Is it because you hate me? Because you hate what I've become?"

"No."

It wasn't hate. It was never hate.

Fear. Discomfort. Distrust. Guilt. But not hate. Never hate.

Nalia sighs and looks into his eyes. "I don't understand you. It hurts me that I brought death into the world when I gave birth to you. I wanted your brother; I didn't want you. But you came anyway."

"It might as well be hate." The pain in his voice is real.

"I hate goodbyes, and pain, and ending. I am magic. I exist to bend the natural rules! To break them when I wish! I was supposed to be the end of endings. But, here you are, with your kindness and suffering. My son, I can't do a thing to stop you, and that goes against who I am. I wish you didn't have to be."

She may as well wish he'd never been born.

Baedrogan pulls his hand away with a grimace. This was the death of his warmth toward her. "All things must end."

"No! Not everything."

Baedrogan turns his back on her. "Everything."

His words are final. Her son disappears.

Nalia sets her jaw and is determined to find a way.

"Mother."

The still whiteness of snow is a shroud on the world, pure and crisp and cold. Even sound was a muffled whisper absorbed by layers upon layers of tiny crystals.

Perhaps if she was mortal the cold would numb what had come to pass.

"Hastriva. You look weak."

The goddess of peace shakes her head and smiles. "When even gods are at war, how else would I look? This winter is the unkindest of all."

"It's merely a season. It will pass."

They sit together, in their own thoughts, sharing sympathy with each other, but there's a sour note that spoils the harmony that should sit between them.

"You're my favorite," Nalia says idly, just to see what her daughter will do.

A laugh comes, unexpectedly bright. "Your favorite what? Favorite of all the other gods? No. Favorite of your children? Hardly. The only favorite of yours is yourself. Even when you see the rest of us, you see a reflection or a deficit of yourself."

"No."

"We're on the eve of battle. You've given all power to Thar and Brin." Hastriva dances in the snow as it falls, lets it collect in her hair. "If I were your favorite, you'd kill me and spare me what's to come."

It's one thing Nalia won't do.

"When this is over," Nalia says, "you'll see. You'll be strong again, and healthy, and your doubts in me will be erased."

"It will never be over. This snow is a death shroud for the entire world, and that's the only time we'll see peace again."

Such a dramatic child. "Even Agruet can't know that. This will be a war unlike any other war, I'm sure, but this is not the end."

"If it is, Mother, just remember I'm the one who stopped

to say goodbye."

"If it is not, daughter, remember who created this all."
Nalia smiled. "How could you doubt my victory? I am magic.
I overcome all."

"Mother!"

She's a stranger to Nalia, but the word bursts forth from
lips that feel like her own. There is so much love it's
impossible to contain.

Even Esier had never said it with so much kindness, hope,
and joy. Nalia's children had used the word as an epithet at its
worst, or an obeisance at its best.

"Look at you, Agrad." Her tone is amused, exasperated.
"You've got stickers in your hair, and enough mud on your
legs to grow your own garden."

"A flower garden?"

"If you'd like."

It's like a dream. Nalia finds herself holding out a flower,
her hand is pudgy and small, and caked in dirt and pollen.
The flower is wilting already, and it's such a common flower
as to be laughable. But, at the same time, the flower is as
beautiful as this mother is.

Trapped again. A new body. A new face. A new human
prison to dwell within.

But this one has a family. This one is loved and cherished
and cared for. Spoiled.

Like Oralan, but with warmth and care and love and
kindness. Oralan's mother had died, and his father had hated

him for that.

The same, but so very different.

Agrad.

This child was named Agrad.

As plain and common a name as the flower he had given this mother. No great heroes had ever possessed such a name. Humble and small, and clearly too common to have been taken by the wizards so far.

Contemptible.

And all Nalia can do is watch, exist, observe. She is still too weak after Doran's death, barely conscious within this new child. She must submit to being embraced, to being coddled, to being bathed by this woman, this mother, this human spellsmith who forces magic into new shapes so crude as to be insulting.

At this age, this Agrad will surely be taken by wizards at any moment and stolen away. Then growing up will be the same as Nalia has come to expect. Lessons and responsibility and cautious fondness and days full of dull drudgery.

With that thought comes unexpected pain.

Nalia has never been mothered before. Has never had her tears gently wiped away by a gentle giant hand. Has never been embraced, cuddled, kissed, and put to bed with the knowledge that tomorrow will be the same if the mother has anything to say.

All she has now is bittersweet pain. This will end, at any day. Any moment. Even knowing that this mothering is for Agrad, and not for her, not for Nalia, she never wants this to end.

For the first time, the goddess of magic understands regret.

Far from Home

Humans are so ephemeral," Meran Alavraneth said with a wistful sigh. "Like flowers, they only grace us for a short time." The elf smiled to himself, smiled to his son, though there was pain in those words. One should not fall in love with a flower.

One should never fall in love with a human.

"She asked me to leave when you were small," Meran added after a moment.

Krecek nodded. "She told me about that," he said. "I was so young that I don't really remember."

To Meran it was only yesterday. It had caused Shelan such pain to watch her husband be youthful, to be eternal, while she faded. In the end she couldn't handle the reminder of her mortality. She had begged him to leave, crying as she did so. *I want you to remember me still beautiful, still strong, still the woman you married.*

Such an odd, unusual, amazingly strong-willed woman. She never saw him again, but he'd watched her. Through magic, he'd gaze upon her, loving her more as she aged. Shelan's beauty had never been mere flesh. Her soul, her kindness, her honor, and her pride were among the things he'd admired about her.

He didn't want to take her pride away, which was the only reason he seemed to acquiesce.

"Thank you for letting me know of her passing."

Krecek nodded. He stood there, waiting for something. It puzzled Meran. What could the boy want, now that his business was done?

A moment of trying to think like a human gave Meran a glimmer of what might be wrong. Shelan had been the boy's only family, his entire world. Where else would he go? What would he do? He was so young. Meran couldn't just turn the boy out into the world.

"I don't have a room for you. This was unexpectedly sudden." Well, Krecek had a tree of his own planted beside Meran's, but it hadn't grown enough to be a home. That would take a century, at least. How old was Krecek? Merely twenty, or forty, or something close to one of those ages.

"Mother was 82," Krecek said. "We both knew the end was coming for years. I was surprised she lasted so long, with such a frail heart."

Was that old for a human? Was that the right age to die?

"She was so young," Meran murmured softly, bowing his head.

"No," Krecek said. His face was a twisted mess of emotions all over the place. Humor, yes, but also irritation and condescension. "She was very old, for a human."

"Was she?" Odd. A mere eight decades? That was considered old? It was hard to wrap his mind around.

"Yes, Father."

I don't want to look at you and grow to hate you. I already feel the envy eating away at me. My hair is going gray, and my breasts have gone flat and are sagging. I hate to look at myself next to you. I just can't —

"Do you know if...did she still love me in the end?"

"Yes."

It was a relief to hear. "Thank you." Time to set that aside, however. "I'm unsure how to treat you. You're so young. Yet,

16

here you are, as tall as I am and twice as old as your mother was when we met. No, more than twice as old."

"I matured almost as quickly as a human, but I haven't aged a day since I reached adulthood. You really haven't been watching over us, have you?"

It was an impossible answer to give. Either one would cause Krecek pain. "I've been busy." A non-answer, but it gave a plausible excuse. "I couldn't risk hurting her by forcing her to see me again. She didn't want me anymore."

"But she did!" The words were full of pain, regret, recrimination, and grief.

Oh.

Oh no.

"Mother missed you," Krecek said. "I know she did. I could see it in her face, hear it in her voice, every day."

"But she never said it." If she'd ever once said the words, he'd have been at her side, instantly. He'd cast the spells himself, just in case. He'd been so hopeful that she would —

"She didn't have to."

Ah, but she did. Didn't she?

Words were binding. Words had meaning. Words were law, for both elves and mages. It was something his son didn't understand. Couldn't understand. For humans, words seemed to be so mutable, so slippery. It's part of what fascinated him about them.

"You look so much like me," Meran murmured. He placed his hand on Krecek's shoulder. "But you're so very human."

Krecek flinched. Pulled away. His face was twisted my hurt and anger.

"It's not an insult. Not from me. Never from me." Meran grabbed Krecek this time, holding both shoulders tight. An

17

explanation needed to be given. "I don't understand you. You don't understand me. I'm merely fascinated to see you with my own eyes, to see who you have become in my absence. You're an amazing child, like a prodigy. So smart for your age. And then, I remember. You were raised by humans. You are fully an adult, completely mature, and I haven't been there for you since you were as tall as my hips. You don't know your own legacy. Fully an adult, and you know nothing of our people. I've failed you, but at least your mother was there to make up for my lack. My son, the human. A being of wonder and delight."

"What was it that Aunt Siv called me?" Krecek looked unimpressed. "Evidence of your perversion, and a stain on the family honor?"

"She is but one elf among many." Meran dropped his hands, despite his words. It was admission of his defeat. "Stay here, with me. I'll prove it. Siv is angry with me, not you. She may never like you, but most others will."

Most, but not all. That much couldn't be helped, but at least elves guarded their tongues and their expressions.

Krecek would be spared from outright expressions of disgust. The Alavraneth name assured that. Siv was the only one would dare to insult Krecek to his face.

"You said you didn't have anywhere for me to sleep."

"No, I said I didn't have a room," Meran said. "You'll sleep in my bed until I've remedied that. It shouldn't take more than a year or so."

"Where will you sleep?"

"Oh, I'll find a spot." It was a short-term inconvenience he wouldn't mind for his own flesh and blood. He felt playful as an idea struck him. When he'd been a child, he'd used magic

18

to camp on the ceiling. An immature waste of magic for any grown elf, but perhaps a bit of childish indulgence would soothe the pain of Shelan's loss. "This is your home now, for as long as you wish to stay."

Siv stared at her brother and trembled with suppressed rage. "You let him stay in your home?"

Humans were thieves. Beggars. Rapists.

Primitive.

Animals.

They smelled bad, behaved worse, and Siv had never met one she couldn't hate.

"You're just asking to be robbed blind, murdered in your sleep, and your whole tree set on fire, aren't you?"

"He's not like that," Meran said. "He's so much like Shelan—"

"Shelan. The woman who broke your heart, stole your child, and raised that child to be exactly like her. You honestly think keeping him now is a good idea?"

Her rage wasn't against Meran. It wasn't even rage against the child.

Siv would never forgive Shelan.

Never.

Shelan and her whole race of —

"You can't blame a child for what their parents have done."

His tone was steel wrapped in velvet, and the words brought Siv short.

"Very well," she said, bowing her head. It was a gesture nearly foreign to her, but for her brother's sake she would do it. "He has one decade to adapt and prove himself. One decade only, or he'll be banished from our lands. And you will share his fate."

It was more than generous of her. The elders had wanted the boy removed immediately, but Siv had been born to the Alavraneth line. On top of it, she had married into a family of nearly equal status. She had the influence to stay their hands.

"Only a decade?" Meran looked pained.

"I'll have to fight the council for that much." She sighed and removed the circlet from her forehead. It was a symbol of her position of a Velhi, for what that was worth these days. "Meran, lay with whoever you want. My want is only for you to be happy. Have all the half-human bastards you wish, and I'll even be proud of them—from afar. I'll bring them gifts if you ask it of me. But this...you're rubbing it in the council's noses. You didn't just bed the woman, you married her. You gave her and her child our family name, and then you let her cast you aside. This is not what an elfin Venhi does. Does Krecek even know who you are? Did Shelan?"

"No," Meran said. "They don't know what it means to be a Venhi or a Velhi. They call us Lord or Lady, and that's all they need to know. Humans of this era wouldn't understand, there have been too many of their generations since...then."

Siv suppressed a sigh. Family or no, she'd burdened him enough with her emotions on the subject. "Be sure he doesn't find out. The elders would take offense if a child of yours behaved as if he were entitled to that honor."

Meran looked at her, silent for a time, and then he nodded. "They were our parents, not his. And I will not walk

20

in their footsteps. He need never know what it means, except that you're powerful and speak for others who are equally powerful. And that you still speak for me."

"You've earned the title, too," Siv said. "You're a Venhi."

He stood. Walked around her imposing desk. Pulled her into a hug.

Siv sighed. Leaned into it.

She loved her little brother. Loved him fiercely and overwhelmingly. For all that he indulged in the strangest things and she couldn't understand him, she just wanted to protect him from a cruel world.

"Don't get your hopes up, brother," she murmured into his shoulder, indulging in free expression while they held each other so close. "Your son is so very human. He may never belong here. I don't want it to kill you when he goes away."

"I'm stronger than that, Siv." Meran took a step back. Smiled. "One decade. In human years, that's long enough. He'll learn. He'll surprise you."

"I hope so."

It amused Krecek greatly to find he now had a tutor.

Fifty-five years, and he was being treated like a slow child now instead of a venerable man. Life was one odd twist after another. Fine. He'd play along. He had nothing to return to, after all.

First, he was taught the two languages of the elves. Sarahalayarahennsava and Mearahennsava, and at least the two had several prefixes and suffixes in common or he would have given up. The northern elves called themselves the Sarahalayarahenn, which meant the free people of the trees. The northern elves called themselves the Mearahenn, which meant the sun-touched people. Right away, Krecek learned the suffix "sava" denoted the language spoken by a people, and "henn" was people. Or, specifically, it meant elves.

According to the elves, they were the only true people.

His tutor, Master Anain, had been scandalized, then amused, when Krecek asked what humans were called in the elf language and then tried to append the "henn" and "sava" suffixes.

"Those do not apply to humans," he said when he finally had his expression fixed once again. "Humans are, if you will pardon my crudity, hardly more than animals. They breed like animals, they smell like animals, and they live with their animals."

"No, they don't," Krecek said. What an odd thing to say.

"They most certainly do," the elf said, straightening. "Horses, chicken, swine, all in the same lot. They sleep with, and have relations with, dogs. The last time I saw a human settlement, the conditions were appalling."

"My mother didn't live like that. I certainly didn't live like that. None of my neighbors were like that, either."

There was a pause. Master Anain's lips pursed. "I was not aware that so much had changed in such a short period of time. Our experiences are obviously different. That does not make humans our equals, however."

That, it seemed, was that.

The lesson continued that day, and when they were finished Krecek wandered to the edge of a lake. It sparkled like glitter, even beneath the surface. The fish that swam within were beautiful, with long trailing fins that made them seem like dancers as they floated and flitted past. Krecek sat on a moss-covered rock that was as soft as any chair. It seemed perfect.

A soft rustle of fabric was the only warning Krecek had that he wasn't alone.

"Master Anain spoke with me after your lessons today."

Krecek looked up at his father. Raised an eyebrow questioningly.

"He said you had an emotional outburst over our language?"

"An outburst?" It took Krecek a moment, and when he realized it must have been about humans not being people, he laughed. "That's considered an emotional outburst?"

"Yes," Meran said, sitting down beside him. "So is this."

It made Krecek laugh harder.

The sound of it startled birds, made the fish dash away, and brought a stillness to the woods. Everything had startled around them.

Meran frowned and made small placating gestures. "Calm yourself. This is behavior unbecoming of our kind in such a public setting."

"Our kind?" The amusement turned sour, curdling in his stomach. "Your kind, Father. I have no kind, no people. Apparently half of me isn't even a person, according to your people."

"That's not true," Meran said. He put a hand on Krecek's arm. "I know that's how some think still, but they're wrong." He fell silent for a few moments, then spoke gently. "Arguing won't change their minds. Prove them wrong by showing

23

them. By learning. By being yourself around them."

"I've tried that," Krecek said. "No one notices, or cares."

"You've tried that with humans. On a human time scale. Here, we are elves. We are blessed by the gods with strong magic, long life, and a love of nature. We don't conquer. We don't impose our changes on the world. We harmonize and blend."

That sounded like a load of horse shit to Krecek. Maybe it was true on the surface, to a degree, but even a month into staying among elves, he knew it wasn't the whole truth. Those words sounded too pretty, too clean, to be the real.

It was almost as if Meran read Krecek's mind. "We do have our flaws, of course. We are slow to accept change. We are stubborn. When we want to affect others, we manipulate our way into it. Elves are insidious. And, if you don't blend in, you are cast aside. Krecek, here in this place you're going to be judged by the subtlest changes of expression. Any child will read your face as if it were made of words. We live by wit and condemn each other to death with nothing more than a gesture." He paused. Smiled. "When we speak, our nuances have nuances. It frightens me, and thrills me, to be this open and plainspoken, even though I trust you won't use this against me. Being this blunt, even to educate you, feels dangerous."

Maybe for an elf it was as blunt as he said. Flowery, still, but a bit more honest. And depressing. "Maybe it was a mistake for me to come here."

"No," Meran said. He clutched both of Krecek's hands in his own.

Meran's delicate fingers were like small cages of steel, wire-thin but unbreakable. Krecek saw his own fingers,

24

slender for a human, but now sausage-like compared to his father's.

"I don't belong."

"I know."

Krecek tried to pull away, but Meran held him fast.

"Listen to me, child. You don't belong. Anywhere. You never will. You shouldn't try to."

That hurt. Like a knife through his heart, the words hit every sore spot that festered in his soul.

"It's not a curse," Meran continued. "It's your gift. It's a blessing from the gods. Stay here long enough to learn from us. Your aunt gave you ten years, but she's old, and set in her ways even for an elf. Siv has never thought for herself. She thinks there's no way you'll learn our ways in such a short time. However, you think like a human. Humans adapt. Humans absorb everything around them, like sponges, and change it all to their liking. So, learn what you can, as swiftly as you can, and prove them wrong."

"Am I that human?" After living his whole life being told he was so much like an elf, it seemed ridiculous.

"To us, you are." Meran smiled, still holding tight. "To me, you look like all the best traits of humanity. The ones I loved your mother so much for. To others, they're going to look for the worst in you to justify their bigotry. You can plant the seeds that will change it. Become like one of us, for a time, and then show them how much greater than both you are."

That was a tall order, Krecek thought. A lot of expectation to put on one person.

"You can do it," Meran said.

"Am I really that easy to read?" It was frustrating.

But, Krecek realized, he was acting frustrated. His lips

were canted to the side. His brow was furrowed. Eyes narrowed. He could feel it, when he thought about it.

"Oh."

Meran finally let go of Krecek's hands. "I'll help as much as I can. I'll ask Master Anain to go easy on you, and remember who you are, so that he can help as well. Don't be overwhelmed. I have faith in you. You are, every bit of you, my son."

Words that Krecek's mother had said, so many times, and they sounded just as sweet from his father's lips. "Thank you."

"You don't mind that I stole your mother's words?"

He'd known? How? But, just as soon as the questions came to mind, he pushed them aside. Schooled his expression.

"I don't mind," he said. "She would have wanted you to have them."

A hint of expression traveled across Meran's face. Shock. Pain. Pride. Something else that was gone too fast to be seen.

"Said like an elf."

Meran sat reluctantly behind his desk in the council hall. Unlike Siv, he hated his position and all the responsibility it entailed. The family name may still command respect, but he'd done everything in his power to diminish that. Deliberately.

Still, once a year there was paperwork. Taxes to be paid. Permissions and licenses to be granted or renewed. Horse shit to be shoveled, as his son would put it. What an amusing phrase. It made him want to live among humans again.

26

Anain walked in with a polite cough. Well, it skirted the edges of polite, but it was still soft enough to be considered an announcement of his presence rather than a declaration of verbal war.

"What did Krecek do, this time?" Meran didn't bother to look up from his task.

"Venhi Delameran, your son is learning surprisingly quickly, as I've said."

Meran set the paper down. Looked up. "And?"

"I'd like to try something...unusual. With your permission, I'd like him to learn magic. Our magic."

Meran blinked. Blinked again.

After all the complaints and ridicule, this was the last thing Meran expected Anain to say.

"For money, or prestige?"

Anain's hand twitched. Lips pursed. Was he offended? Too bad. Meran wanted to get to the heart of the matter, and his temper was short today.

"Curiosity. I thought someone more talented than I am should be the one to handle the task."

That was a surprise.

"Did you have someone in mind?"

"No, Venhi Delameran."

Another surprise. It was a genuine request, not a bid to put someone else in a higher position.

"It's been only a year. He reads our language well enough to understand our tomes?"

Anain smiled. Proud. "With a minimum of aid, yes."

"I will find him a mentor," Meran said. "Well done."

Anain bowed, left, and Meran was left alone with his own sense of pride.

27

Nine years to go. Would Siv be pleased? Or furious?

"Your aunt is coming to dinner tonight."

Krecek nodded, once, careful not to freeze in place or scowl or a thousand other things that would give away his distaste. "Aunt Siv?"

"She is your only aunt that I am aware of." There was enough amusement in Meran's voice that he might as well have laughed aloud. "She'll be here soon, so put on the blue robes with the gray trim. It will either impress her or irritate her, and I'd like to see which."

"Why would it do either?" He paused, knowing that too little curiosity here would make him seem like he was hiding something. It was exhausting living like this, but he'd adjusted. Adapted. As Meran said he would.

The corners of Meran's eyes pinched together, and they twinkled in the light. "Your grandfather favored those colors. I'd like to remind her of something."

Krecek opened his mouth to ask what, but a pointedly raised eyebrow along with a lift of the head was enough to stop him. This was as much as his father was going to explain.

Fine. Clothes. The only chance he'd have at an answer was if he did as his father requested. He put on the mage robes, still new and not entirely earned yet. It amused Krecek to think of himself as a mage. Before his mother's death, he'd been a gardener. The only spells he'd cast were the ones he read straight from a book to check for life in a seed, or extend a flower's life. It's all the humans had trusted him with, and that had been enough.

Now, here he was, learning magic from an ancient elven mage. Wearing elven mage robes. Living the life of an elven lord...almost.

Almost.

Krecek looked himself over in the mirror. He'd never have a silver circlet like his father. That was reserved for the lords, the Venhai, and Krecek would never have that honor. He assumed it was because of his human heritage, though no one would say it aloud.

What he didn't set aside was that his father had told him he would never fit in. Yet, Aunt Siv had said he must fit in, within a decade, or be exiled. The contradiction bothered him less and less as time went on, but when he looked in the mirror the reminder stared him in the eye. For an elf, he was tall. For a human he was short. For an elf, he was stocky. For a human he was nearly emaciated. He would always be some blur in between the two.

There was nothing he could do about it. Whatever the eventual outcome, he learned.

When Siv arrived he walked out, bowed to her. "Velhai Vanosiv," he said formally, title and full first name. The names were never to be spoken around outsiders, but at some point after the second year of learning magic he'd been pulled aside and taught this etiquette. He smiled, just a touch, and forced warmth into his voice. "It's good to see you again, Aunt Siv."

Her slight smile matched his exactly. "Nephew," she said. Her eyes trailed over him, taking in his robes, and the smile disappeared. "Your studies are that far advanced already? No one informed me. I'd have sent a gift."

"No," Krecek said, bowing his head. "I think this is Father's way of informing you? It will be a few more weeks, at least, before I'm ready for the test."

"Weeks?"

Meran nodded. "I wanted you to see this before anyone else. He's close enough that he deserves to wear the robes, at least in the comfort of home."

Her eyes went wide for a moment, then narrowed as she turned her attention to Meran. "It's only been five years!" Her voice was shrill, choked with emotion.

"Don't worry, Siv. He still doesn't fit in. But, like a human, he's a master of pretending." The undertones, the bitter sarcasm that laced every word, would have escaped Krecek's attention before. Now it was a slap across the face, a nasty rebuke for all the doubts Siv had voiced before.

Krecek shifted his weight from one foot to another. He didn't like being a pawn played between the two of them.

"Father, I'm not pretending. I'm learning."

Neither Siv nor Meran liked that.

It was a small rebellion against them both, and it felt good.

"Aunt Siv was right. I'll never belong here. Father, you even said that was my gift." Krecek smiled as placidly as he could make it. "I don't plan on staying here forever. I want to learn as much as I can and then leave. I'll visit if I'm allowed, because it is beautiful and peaceful here. The thing is, I can tell I'm a point of contention. Not just between the two of you, but among others as well. I'm not welcome here. It's fine. But I'd like to finish learning magic, if it won't cause too much of a problem."

They both looked as if they were made of marble by the

30

time he stopped talking.

"You'd be willing to say that to the council?" Siv's shoulders were relaxing. Not triumph, but a very cautious realization that she'd come out of this with what she wanted.

"Of course," Krecek said. "Formally, properly, and without reservation."

"You don't have to do that," Meran said quickly.

Krecek nodded. He knew that, understood the trap Meran was warning him against, and simply didn't care. "If it will keep peace, and make others feel more at ease, it's fine." He paused, shifted weight from one foot to another again, considering his next words. "You both still treat me like an unpredictable and immature child. My childhood friends have grandchildren. I spent a lot of time working with my hands, doing things that require patience and attention to detail. It's how I made a living before I came here."

Siv fluttered her hands in a gesture of confusion, then resignation. "You're right. I haven't treated you fairly at all. I have my reasons."

Meran nodded, and if there was any other expression to accompany that gesture it was too subtle for Krecek to catch.

"I've made a decision." Siv's voice was soft, contemplative, which spoke of an idea she'd mulled over but had only just come to a conclusion on. "I'm going to sponsor you at a university far from here. It's in a human city, but that's not the reason I'd like to send you there. An elf teaches there who is more adept in the arts than anyone here who would be willing to teach you. You can wait out your time here, and press your welcome, or you can leave sooner and engender some measure of good will. The elders would appreciate the latter and perhaps welcome you in the future if you do."

"You're sending him away?" Meran took a step forward.

Siv shook her head. "No." She paused. Spread her hands out in front of her in a sort of surrender. "Maybe. I don't know." Her body language was suddenly all over the place, open and easy to read, but chaotic. "Strictly as family, I hadn't planned to offer this. Meran, I'm absolutely furious with you. You've put me in an impossible position with this move. But I honestly think this is what's best for the boy." She paused for a beat to look Krecek over. "Pardon me, for this grown man who should still be a boy but isn't. Our society isn't ready for this sort of upheaval, but it's not fair to exclude him from his birthright simply because you made some terrible decisions, brother." She took a deep breath, still frowning, obviously upset, and took a step away. "You keep pushing me. I know why you chose those colors for him. Message received. He is his own person. Hear the message for yourself. I am too upset to dine with you. Good evening."

She turned abruptly and left.

Meran walked over and flumped down on the couch.

Now THAT was an emotional outburst.

For an elf, it was akin to a screaming match.

All done at a volume that humans would consider a whisper.

Krecek sat down next to Meran. "My fault?"

"No," Meran said softly. "You did well tonight and guarded your emotions well. I'm sorry. I still think of you as a child, and I used you like one tonight. You're not."

Krecek leaned back. Shook his head. "Mother treated me like a child, too. Well, until the end. I think that's just how parents treat their children despite the years."

"Did she?"

32

There was a look in Meran's eyes. An expression Krecek had seen, but never noticed. Never thought about.

After all this time getting to know his father, Krecek finally realized what it was.

"You miss her."

The words were a thoughtless statement, blurted out tactlessly. He wished he could take them back, because Meran looked like he'd been punched in the gut.

Krecek saw tears in Meran's eyes before he turned away.

"Of course I do."

Of course he did.

It was so easy to think of elves as cold and unfeeling, when their expressions betrayed nothing but what they chose to show the world.

It was only after years of wearing the same masks that Krecek realized. Their expressions, their posture, were all language. A means of communication. They whispered instead of shouting, but it didn't mean they had no voice.

When Siv had said "strictly as family" her body language had changed. She'd opened up. She'd trusted them with the truth of herself.

And Meran had taken her lead. Was still open. Still raw.

Had Meran kept his expressions closed and careful because he was setting an example?

Maybe...

"If you live where people scream all the time, you stop hearing whispers," Krecek murmured to himself.

Meran froze. Nodded after a moment. "Shelan and I understood each other, I thought. I took her at face value, listening to her voice as a human instead of her body, like an elf. When you came here and told me she'd wanted me around...that she didn't have to say it...I thought back. What if you're right? What if I hurt her by taking her at her words? I thought I was respecting her and the ways of her people. But what if you're right?"

He was crying. Krecek couldn't see it, because Meran's head was still turned away. As if showing so much emotion was embarrassing. Or, no, what if he was sparing Krecek from being overwhelmed? What if weeping openly was akin to screaming into someone's ear.

"It's okay," Krecek said. He pulled his father in for a hug, to hold him and comfort him. "You can feel whatever you feel. It's like carrying a table. It's large and bulky. You can do it alone, but it's easier together." There were tears of his own rising, for his own loss, but also in sympathy for what his father must have been going through silently all this time. For the tragedy of thinking they'd understood each other, but they'd only just missed. "I miss her, too. Every day. Mother was my world, and the only person who accepted me for who I am. You won't crush me under the weight of your grief on top of mine. We can carry it together."

It was an awkward metaphor, but Meran seemed to understand. He melted into Krecek's arms and cried until the pain quieted.

And then, without pretense, they talked through the night. They shared stories of things they had seen or been through, wisdom and perspective from their vastly different lives, and a familial love despite spending so long estranged.

Meran stood at the edge of the forest, hesitated. "I could go the rest of the way with you," he said. "Just let me get my horse."

"I have a map," Krecek said. "I'll find my way." He patted his horse, soothing him in the misty morning air. "Don't worry, I'll find my way back someday, too."

"Who said I was worried?" He was nearly to the point of laughter. "I just want to get away from Siv for a while. She'll be impossible now that you're gone."

It was a joke, but it wasn't a lie. He'd walk with Krecek around the world, if he were welcome, but Meran knew where not to overstep. They'd talked quite a bit in the last few months.

They'd come to an understanding.

"You're always welcome to visit me."

Krecek's words hung in the air.

The invitation Meran had always wanted.

"I will," he promised. "I don't know when, but I will."

Meran found himself in a very tight, very human embrace. It felt good and right.

"I'll miss you," they both said.

They laughed.

Krecek was gone. A figure in blue and silver robes, now earned, winding along the open road. And then, the landscape swallowed him.

The silence of home would be different now. He'd heard the halls filled with laughter and shouts. He'd seen anger and grief and joy invade his sanctum and make the place their own.

It would be lonelier, now.

But more than ever, he knew he wasn't alone. Meran

knew in his bones he had a family, a real and true family, no matter how far away.

Prelude

The tavern was dark, the company unsavory. Within the great room, the air was heavy with the scent of pipes and drink and an honest day's sweat. At the hearth sat a small band of minstrels, playing for their night's lodging.

Most important was the music.

The musicians themselves weren't particularly talented. There was no supernatural nudge toward perfection or anything of the sort. That, in Baedrogan's opinion, was the largest part of the appeal. They were living their short, mortal years in service to making the lives of those around them more tolerable. What could be more noble? The god of death smiled to himself at the pleasure of such ephemeral and emotional entertainments.

"They're too young," Agruet grumbled in a low voice beside him.

Baedrogan narrowed his eyes, glaring momentarily at his brother. Did his twin have no ears? No heart? No soul? Why would he speak in the middle of a performance? Why would he be so crass as to interrupt the song?

At least the pair of gods were off to the side where the musicians wouldn't be offended or distracted. It would have really annoyed Baedrogan to stand and apologize for his brother's lack of manners.

"It goes against my plan." Agruet tapped his fingers on the table, ignoring the cadence set by the drums.

"Don't lay the blame on me," Baedrogan muttered, irritated enough to reply mid-song. If Agruet wanted to talk about this now, he might as well go along and get it over with. "You're the one who asked favors from the forces of chaos. I've merely adjusted to what followed."

Agruet scowled.

"Give it time and patience. It will unfold in accordance with the grander scheme of things." It wasn't often that Baedrogan had a secret his brother didn't know. It brought him no real pleasure. Well, no, it did make him feel momentarily smug, which was its own sort of joy. But they were partners, not adversaries in this venture. "I had contingency plans, same as you."

"You're skirting a line," Agruet snapped. "Just make sure the others don't find out."

"Isn't that your job, brother?"

Agruet threw Baedrogan a withering glance and opened his mouth to reply, but the music ended. Baedrogan held up a hand, silencing Agruet before he could answer. He applauded the musicians as they stood to take a break. People began milling around, talking, filling the tavern with a low rumble instead of the lively tunes of before.

Agruet raised an eyebrow, then gestured to the door. It was a good idea, Baedrogan realized. Privacy would make the discussion they needed to have easier.

The air outside was cool, and a mist was forming along the ground. The sweet perfume of decaying leaves, hearth smoke, and heavy moisture hung on the autumn air. Overripe fruits fallen at the base of trees, and fields left fallow ahead of the first frost added to the cacophony of scents. This was Baedrogan's favorite season, as everything was preparing for dormancy, feeling the impending winter, but had not yet succumbed.

"I can't keep every secret on my own, you know," Agruet grumbled. "There are limits to even my power."

"Relax. She who aids us is keeping the others distracted. You created the plan; we're just following it."

"What's left of my plan." Agruet guided them a few steps into a copse of nearby trees. He sighed in an uncharacteristic moment of defeat. "When you work with chaos, chaos ensues. I just hope enough is left of my ideas that we can pull it off. Both sides of it all."

Baedrogan nodded. "The next step is almost upon us."

Agruet stepped in close, eyes narrowed. "You're awfully confident, all things considered. How are two mere children going to start a war for us? How could they possibly win such a war?"

"The girl is talented. The boy is young. They're human." Baedrogan gestured, as if that would explain all. "I know that focusing on the girl was a mere contingency plan, but don't let that concern you. She was integral to my part of the plan even before things fell apart."

"I don't like it going this direction," Agruet shook his head. "It's needlessly cruel. The boy should have been spared what's to come."

"On that we agree," Baedrogan said. "I gave them every chance, but I'm not surprised by their decision. You may understand secrecy and know more about the big picture than anyone, but I know how people react to the prospect of death. They were bound to choose the life of their son over their own lives." He leaned against a tree and stared off in the distance. "Sparing the boy's life may make some of this easier than sparing his suffering. The horror of it all will draw more sympathy."

Agruet lapsed into silence for a few moments, looking Baedrogan over thoughtfully as he did. "Look how out of touch I've become." He let out a bitter laugh. "Out of step with mortal motivations. This is why the war must come. Now, before I've lost it all."

Baedrogan opened his mouth to reply, but he stopped as he became aware that someone approached. The rustle of dead leaves was hushed, but discernable to the pair of gods. It was a sound that would not have been caught by most mortals. Elves were adept at stealth. The two turned, waiting in expectant silence.

"My lords," the elf said, gracefully slipping to his knees in obeisance as soon as he was in view.

Agruet gestured him toward them. "You're late."

The elf nodded, but offered no excuse. "I am."

"What's this?" Baedrogan demanded.

"My own contingency plan." Agruet smiled a grim, tight-lipped smile. "He lives in Anogrin. He can guide the girl, if need be."

Baedrogan glowered. "It won't be necessary. I've told you—"

"I've already taught him the spell."

So. That was that. A mortal already knew. A sense of inevitability settled in Baedrogan's bones, and after a moment he nodded. "I see. It seems that one way or another, these things shall come to pass."

"I wouldn't breathe a word of it without your leave," the elf said. "I swear it."

This was rewarded by Agruet grasping the elf's hand with the comfortable familiarity of an old lover. "It's why I trust you with it."

"Ah, brother, you're going to be the death of us all." Baedrogan slumped in defeat.

"Only if everything goes right."

Smoke and Mirrors

Anogrin was beautiful in winter.

At least, Fadal thought it was, and it had always been her favorite season. Crisp snow clung to tree boughs, to rooftops, making the already glowing city sparkle. Everything looked clean and fresh from her vantage at the castle window.

"If I could capture this feeling in a spell, I could sell it on every street corner and make a fortune from it," she said.

From the other side of the room, Torba laughed. "Selling emotions, now, hm? Isn't that dangerous?"

"It's why I said, 'if I could'. I'm not stupid enough to actually try it." Fadal rubbed her belly, a motion she'd taken up in the last few weeks of her pregnancy. "There's a reason that even the old gods forbade that magic. Society would collapse if we could just cast a spell and feel happy and at peace without earning it."

Silence filled the room for a few moments. Torba looked at his wife, brows knit together and a frown tugging at the corners of his mouth. He then carefully looked around the room. "The pregnancy must have you addled. Talking about old gods as if any of their teachings held wisdom. You're going to get us removed from our positions talking like that."

Fadal lost every trace of the peace she'd found while gazing across the landscape. As a spellsmith, she knew better. She knew what sorts of spells were tossed casually around in this place. She swallowed, hard, wrapped her arms around herself as if she could give her unborn baby a hug.

Smile, she reminded herself silently, *maybe no one's watching, maybe they are, but act like everything's fine.*

"I'm sure even Lord Ceolwyn would agree to the wisdom of that one admonition," Fadal said, more for the sake of anyone potentially listening than for her husband's peace of mind. "Not that it's important. Just an idle thought." The laugh that followed was meant to be a light admission of her foolishness, but it sounded hollow and forced even to her own ears.

Torba set aside his book and walked over to her, wrapped his arms around her from behind, hid his face in her hair. "I know why you're thinking of the old gods right now. I understand. But, it might be a false alarm. The baby might just be very talented. We won't know until it's been born."

She nodded, slipping her eyes closed. "I'm probably worried for nothing."

"Of all the women in all the world carrying future mages and spellsmiths, only one right now is carrying an elemental." He kissed her on the cheek.

"Only one?" Fadal twisted to look into his face, questioning.

"I just heard the news today," Torba said. "They found Eudwyn a few days ago in a small village a day's ride from Naeriloran. A human girl, this time."

"And Uriwyn was reborn last year." Fadal leaned back against Torba. "That leaves Verwyn." It wasn't comforting in the least, even if it reduced the odds that their already strongly magical baby would be an elemental. "I can't even imagine, bringing another Doran Verwyn into the world. He grabbed me once at a party, kissed me, and told me to meet him upstairs." The memory was a traumatic one that brought a full-body shudder over her. "I was terrified not to, but then he never showed up. Even with that close of a call I had crying fits for a week." She stared outside again, trying to regain the peace she'd felt before, but that had been erased at the thought she might have more to do with Verwyn no matter what face he wore. "Torba, I can't do this. I can't. If my baby's Verwyn I can't. They'll turn him into a monster."

"Shhh," he held her close, rocked her back and forth. "It's an honor to give birth to a wizard. We'll be favored even more than we are now, given lands and titles and respect. We'll want for nothing. Remember that."

Fadal nodded, stifling her tears. This was the way of things. It was all for the best. It would all work out fine. "It's an honor to be chosen," she whispered.

Even if it meant giving up their child. It was just one child among many they might someday have.

One special, precious child she'd been hoping to have for years.

"The pregnancy just has me emotional," she assured her husband, assured anyone who might by chance listen in on them, and vowed to keep silent from that point on.

She went on with her life, trying not to think about the possibility day to day.

After all, Fadal Leyfraiin was a master spellsmith already. She was young and respected and powerful enough to be on staff in Anogrin, working directly with Lord Ceolwyn, so she knew a thing or two about keeping her emotions in check. More than that she knew how to keep herself busy and distracted. Pregnancy made it harder, true, but not impossible. Every day she did her job with peace and grace and precision.

Every night she fell asleep with tears and terror and worry.

"What if the baby really is Verwyn?" Fadal asked herself silently in the darkness, always in the darkness, always when she was alone, when no one could answer.

Wandering the halls, insomnia building, Torba asked the same. "What if our baby really is Verwyn?"

They'd been so thrilled after trying so long, trying so hard, just for one child. One year of marriage and it was a relief that they were still free to pursue magic without distraction. Two and three years in they began to question, but they were young and had the whole world ahead of them, they weren't trying hard, probably distracted, probably just didn't have time in those magical windows when life could begin.

Five years married and Torba was convinced he'd done something wrong, was damaged by a childhood illness, something. He quietly gave up, convinced it would never happen. Some couples just weren't blessed and as soon as the thought of being blessed occurred to him he longed for the days when he could pray to some pagan god to fix this or a god to rail against and blame or at least someone he could pray to who would listen and give comfort or a sense of purpose or something.

In the beginning they worked with Lord Ceolwyn, but that did not make them friends. When they became friends with Lord Ceolwyn, they didn't want to impose on such a busy man. A year ago they heard about another couple who begged a different wizard for a child and were granted some half-human thing that they thought had been born dead or dying because even its skin was so blue. There were whispers that the child was a monster, incapable of love, and Torba didn't want to put Fadal through an ordeal like that after all they'd already been through.

As they approached six years of being a family of two Torba considered asking anyway. Lord Ceolwyn was older, wiser, and stronger than all the other wizards. It might be worth the risk, and Lord Ceolwyn could learn from the other wizard's mistakes. Then Fadal gave him the good news, and asking for help hadn't been necessary.

A sound pulled Fadal from his thoughts.

"Someone's baby will be Verwyn," came a reply from the shadows. "Why fret that it could be yours?"

This is why Torba had chided Fadal for speaking her mind. This exactly. Wizards had a way of knowing, of being unseen, of sneaking up on a person who thought they were alone.

"Lord Lorwyn, I didn't see you there," Torba said, bowing low and clenching his hands together to keep them from trembling. "It was just idle musing on my part, sir." At least it wasn't Ceolwyn, at least it wasn't Ceolwyn, at least —

"You sounded worried or scared, not idle," Lorwyn said. He stepped closer, into the light, and circled Torba for a few moments, as if he were prey. "You're Master Leyfraiin, aren't you? Your wife is Fadal? The charming lady I met the other day?"

"Yes, sir."

"What is it that you fear about this child of yours?"

"It's not a fear, sir!" Torba straightened, the lie coming out automatically. He'd almost convinced himself he was not afraid by repeating it so many times.

Lorwyn cocked his head to the side, gaze half-lidded and contemplative. "If the child is Verwyn, a lot would change for you and your wife. The two of you are such well-known spellsmiths, with such a reputation that any wizard would beg you to join their staff." Lorwyn paused a moment, then nodded to himself as if he'd made a decision. "If the child is Verwyn, allow me to be the first to extend an offer. You must know that Ceolwyn traditionally takes Verwyn as his apprentice. For a time your child would be shuffled around to the different countries, before the apprenticeship would begin. That means that you two would be, as well." He tapped his lower lip with a finger and frowned. "What an inconvenience, making sure you never saw your only child again."

"Only?"

Lorwyn nodded. "I hate to be the one to tell you this. Fadal possesses a defect in her body. It's the type that most healers wouldn't notice. The two of you have had many false starts, miscarriages, over the years, yes?" He waited until Torba nodded to continue. "What holds this baby in, makes it thrive instead of fail, is that it's nigh impossible to kill a wizard, even before they're born."

All the blood drained to Torba's feet and his eyes were wide as saucers. "It is Verwyn. Who else knows?"

"Just you. Just me," Lorwyn said. "For now, at least. The others will know the moment the baby is born."

"No," Torba whispered.

"The babe will have two seasons to suckle, and then the

47

two of you will never see him again."

"Fadal is worried," Torba said quickly. "What if the baby grows up to be a hedonist and warmonger like Doran Verwyn was?"

"The chances of that are high," Lorwyn said. He took a step back and leaned against the wall. "If your baby is raised the same way Doran was."

"You mean, if his apprenticeship is the same? If tradition is followed? What about every other Verwyn? Were they the same?"

"Oralan, the first born to be Verwyn, wasn't," Lorwyn said gently. "He was my best friend, when we were young. We were each raised by our parents. We went to war, but only to ensure we would be given our due. Not out of boredom or madness or greed."

"Was Oralan a good man his whole life, then?" Torba found himself reluctantly fascinated by the story this wizard was weaving.

"No," Lorwyn answered. "He had a lot to overcome. Oralan wasn't raised in a loving home, the way I was. He did his best, but he was broken to begin with." The wizard leaned close and offered a comforting hand on Torba's shoulder. "Verwyn has a good soul, and an innate kindness, despite the reputation he's earned the last few times he's been alive."

Torba opened his mouth to ask more questions, to learn more about the kind of person his future child once was, but he stopped himself. "No. Forget I asked anything. It doesn't matter. We don't have any choice in how the child will be raised."

"If you did, though, would you take the child and run?"

Torba fell silent, tempted by the thought. They could live

normal lives. He and Fadal could raise an elemental child, because they understood magic on such a deep and grand scale. They could keep even a powerful child in check, raise him right, teach him to be better than the others had been...

They could be examples of how wizards could be, if raised correctly. If they were raised with love.

It took a few moments, but finally Torba nodded, once.

"Even though you know you'll be executed if you're caught."

"I know. But I'd do anything for my son."

Lorwyn grinned. "You'll have to do exactly what I say." His instructions followed, simple but imperative. The wizard ended with, "Find a small town to hide in. Go to Verwyn, Eudwyn, Uriwyn, or Lorwyn. In Eudwyn or Uriwyn, you can hide yourselves without another wizard actively searching their own lands for a few years. If you hide in Verwyn, there will never be a wizard to seek him out, but at puberty his emotions will be joined with the land and could give him away. If you go to Lorwyn I will help hide you as long as I can, but there are other risks there. That choice, at least, is yours."

"Why would you help us with this?"

"My reasons are my own." He leaned in. "I'm sure I don't have to say this, but I don't like to leave too much to chance. Don't breathe a word of this to anyone, not even your wife, until I say so." He paused. Chuckled. "Or do. It'll be your life, not mine. I'm giving advice, not orders today."

Lorwyn strolled away casually while Torba took deep breaths to try to quell his fears.

The room was warm despite the winter winds outside. Fadal was exhausted, but the baby's cry was healthy and loud and filled the entire room.

She barely had time to pull up a blanket for the sake of modesty before the door burst open.

"It's a boy," Mistress Phae, the midwife, said with her gentle voice and soothing tones.

Fadal leaned back. She'd known it was a boy already.

Just as she already also knew —

"It's him. It's Verwyn."

Mistress Phae's next words weren't so gentle. "The mother touches first, I don't care who you are."

There were five of them in the room. Five wizards. Name of the gods, why? Why couldn't she have even the first moments alone, to pretend at least?

The baby boy was placed on her chest, still screaming at the injustice of all this light and air and space around him.

"Push again, dear. There you go. This one will be easier, but you still must push it out."

Fadal's arms were empty as she delivered the afterbirth. Someone had taken the baby.

"There you go," Mistress Phae repeated. "Relax. Everything's fine."

Torba took Fadal's hand. He looked grim, but still accomplished. "You did it," he said.

"I wish I hadn't," she whispered, looking over at the wizards who held the babe, stood around and cooed and laughed and made very pleased faces.

50

"We've never seen him so young, so fresh," Lady Kaelwyn said.

"His hair is as black as mine is white," Lord Ceolwyn laughed, touching the tiny hand, examining the miniature fingernails with awe.

Torba kissed Fadal's head. "Don't wish that, my dearest. Don't. It will be fine. Now pretend."

Lord Lorwyn looked over, met Fadal's eyes, then looked away.

"I'll be fine," she said as she put on her bravest face and smile. "Emotional from all the effort is all. It's natural, right? To be overwhelmed?"

Lord Ceolwyn brought the baby back over. "Thank you, Fadal. You've given us a great gift."

Lady Maelwyn nodded, patted Fadal on the shoulder. "We've never had a chance before to be close to the mother of one of our own."

The other wizard, Lord Aledwyn, patted the baby on the head and left without a word.

"We should make announcements," Lady Kaelwyn said as she swept grandly out of the room.

Fadal found herself with her arms full of the squirming little boy, diapered and dressed and fussing, Torba seated beside her, and Lord Lorwyn watching them both.

"Have you chosen a name?"

"Are we even allowed to?" Fadal's bitterness crept into her voice despite herself.

"You'll have to call him something." Lorwyn shrugged.

Torba shook his head. "We haven't been able to decide. It's hard to choose, knowing who he is, what he'll be."

"May I make a suggestion?"

Fadal looked at Lord Lorwyn, skeptical, but nodded.

"I'd be honored if you'd name him after a friend." Lord Lorwyn's mouth twisted into a playful grin. "Someone I've known all my life. Agrad."

"It's a nice name," Torba said, diplomatically.

"It's rather common for a wizard, isn't it? Wasn't there already one with that name? Long ago? Now half the children out there have a name similar."

"Her name was Agret Draewyn," Lorwyn said. "And you were named after a Draewyn, too, Fadal."

Fadal nodded. "That's probably why I've heard the name. My parents were from Draewyn. Moved here when I was born." She found herself distracted immediately, because the baby had grabbed onto one of her fingers with a surprisingly strong grip, and he'd gone quiet.

Torba brushed hair from Fadal's face, smiling. "It's a perfect name, really. It will keep him humble, and it won't stand out."

"It will help him keep his secrets," Lorwyn said. "One caution. Don't tell the others his name."

Fadal's head snapped up. "What?"

"You don't want them to find you," Lorwyn chuckled. "Tell her now. They'll be distracted." Lorwyn took a step backward, toward the door. "Fortune upon you both. Goodbye."

Fadal looked up at Torba, tears in her eyes. "What was that about?"

"We're leaving. The three of us. As soon as you've recovered. I have friends in Lorwyn, in a town called Lesser Stonegore. We'll hide. We'll raise Agrad as our own son. Can you stay here a fortnight? Can you lie to the wizards for that

52

long?"

"Yes," she sobbed. "I finally get a child of my own. My little Agrad...my little secret..."

From Darkness

There are monsters in the dark."

"Are there?" Modarian looked up from his book, sticking a finger in it to keep his place as he slowly closed it. "What sorts of monsters?"

Shaelek, at five years old, spread her arms wide. "Big ones!" Her eyes went wide, and she puffed out her cheeks to further emphasize their size. "They're fuzzy and they know my name, and when the wind is blowing they tell me to go outside, even when you say not to. They're naughty."

"They're just big? How do you know they're monsters?"

"Because they go 'RAWR!' at me all the time."

It brought Modarian to a pause. Imagination? It could be. It probably was. But, what if...?

"Are they scary monsters?"

Shaelek sat down next to Modarian and tilted her head. Her eyes were narrow, giving the question quite a bit of consideration.

"They can't hurt me," the child said, words measured.

Of course not. She was a wizard born, though still mostly untrained. Shaelek had the raw power to defend herself from nearly anything.

"But, do they scare you?"

She shook her head, but there was a hesitation to the action that revealed her lie.

"Do they scare you?" Shaelek turned the question back on Modarian.

It would be easy to scoff and point out that of course they didn't, because he'd never even seen them. They were

54

creations of her imagination, not his. And, of course, he was a wizard of great power and centuries of experience.

However, she wasn't actually asking if her monsters scared him. She was asking for permission to admit that she was afraid. He could see it in her eyes, feel it in her trembling soul, and knew he owed the girl more than an easy answer.

"There are many things that scare me," he said, hand on her shoulder, smile traced upon his lips. "Even with all the magic and knowledge I've been given, I get scared. I know the monsters can't hurt me, but sometimes I can't stop monsters from hurting someone else, and that scares me the most."

"Like if they hurt me?"

Modarian nodded.

Shaelek scowled and looked down at her lap. "They told me I'm a bad girl. That I'd get in trouble." The vehemence of her tone took Modarian aback, but he didn't have a reply before her shoulders slumped, and she continued in a whisper. "They only scare me at bedtime, when I'm all alone. Because I can't tell them to stop it. I have to settle down and go to sleep."

"Is that when they tell you to go outside?"

Another pause. Hesitation. And then, a reluctant nod.

Finally, "I went outside."

"What happened?" Modarian wasn't in the least surprised. She was a precocious child, and too curious for her own good. He knew this already.

"They said, 'RAWR!' It was scary. But they couldn't hurt me, so I went back to bed. And now they say I'm in trouble."

Modarian frowned. "You did disobey my rule to stay inside when it's dark. It's not behavior to be rewarded. However, considering the circumstances, you're not in trouble this time." He ruffled her hair and she smiled up at him. "I'd like to meet these monsters, though."

Don't.

The single word dominated his mind; an alien thought interjecting itself into his consciousness. With it came a stab of fear.

At the same time, Shaelek shook her head. "I don't think they'd let you. They only come when I'm alone."

"I see."

He'd still thought they were imaginary monsters until the voice of the other, of the dead god who shared his soul, had spoken up. Modarian looked Shaelek over more closely now, trying to come up with an answer that would keep her from being tormented at night by whatever force this may be. He moved to set his book aside —

The book.

It was a book of ancient spells, and the one he'd been looking at had been a spell to cast light to illuminate your enemies in battle to make them easier to strike.

The monsters only came at night, in the dark.

The spell in the book was impractical, and too complicated for a wriggling little girl, but it gave Modarian an idea.

"Would you like to learn a new trick?"

Shaelek looked up. Smiled. She hadn't had much patience for learning spells when he'd started teaching the basics a year ago. Tricks, on the other hand, had caught her attention. Making it sound slightly forbidden, just a bit naughty, and much more enticing was the way to hold her attention. So began her magic education, with mischief the goal instead of mastery.

"What kind of trick?"

Modarian held out his hands, palms together, side by side. As he drew them apart a glowing ball formed in the space between them. It was a faint glimmer, barely enough to be seen in full daylight. His goal was that the light had to be dim enough to sleep by, but bright enough to bring her peace.

"Teach me, teach me!" Shaelek demanded, holding out her hands.

"It's hard," he warned her. "You have to concentrate on being gentle. If you don't, the light will die." He demonstrated by putting too much energy into the spell. Instantly it flashed and burned itself out. "But, I think it will be enough to keep your monsters away."

"It will," she said, voice steady and expression determined. "Show me."

It was supposed to be a day of rest, but teaching moments sometimes presented themselves outside of rigid schedules. Modarian didn't mind the disruption in the least. They spent the day together on the spell, until Shaelek could do it on her own.

Her nanny, Mistress Esandir, cleared her throat in the doorway many hours later. "I know that matters of magic are all important to wizards like you, Lord Lorwyn, but Lady Eudwyn still has a bedtime. You had your way with eating your meals in the study, but now I must insist."

"Quite right," Modarian said, ready and eager for peace and quiet, but pretending reluctance so Shaelek wouldn't be upset. "Place the light on your headboard, and it will keep you safe all night. Peace upon you."

"Peace upon you," Shaelek repeated as she gave Modarian a hug goodnight. "Thank you, Modarian. You're my favorite wizard ever. I hope I get to apprentice with you when I'm big."

She ran out of the room, Mistress Esandir quick to follow, leaving Modarian speechless. Such a sweet statement, like she was saying "I love you" to a parent. But new wizards didn't have that anymore. He wondered if she even knew the words.

Yes. He'd take her as his apprentice. He'd avoided it for previous Eudwyn children, because he was avoiding unpleasant memories from both this lifetime and the last. But yes, it was time.

Modarian nodded to himself and picked up the book once again. Shaelek would be the last Eudwyn child, after all. It was the only chance he'd get.

Still Waters

I – Childhood

It's funny how the biggest changes in life come in sudden moments.

Dealing with those moments can last a lifetime.

My parents, Lord and Lady Ronar, were my world when I was little. They loved and cherished me. The castle would always be my home.

Or so I believed.

The castle was not theirs.

The title of Lord and Lady were not actually theirs, either, but granted to them as ambassadors. I picked that much up from what people would say and innocent questions I had. The only lord of this castle was Lord Ceolwyn, and he treated my parents nearly as equals within his own home. We were honored guests, and I was special.

This isn't the story of how I was a pampered princeling in a wizard's castle, however. In the grand scheme of things, this was a blink of an eye. I remember when I was adored by all I met, but only barely.

I don't know who my parents were ambassadors for or where they were from. There's a lot I don't know about them. Where they came from, or how they came to keep such close company with wizards.

I was almost five when my mother gave birth to my little sister and life as I knew it changed.

"She has black hair," my father stepped out of the birthing

room with a relieved sigh. "Thank all the gods and wizards. We have a child at last."

The midwife clucked from where she stood behind him. "You should watch what you say around children. They hear more than you know. You don't want to hurt the boy."

"What? Ysili?" He glanced at me and scoffed. "He's no child of mine, and now I'm not beholden to him at all. We have a child, Mistress Phae!" A manic grin grew across his face. "A real child, not some creature the wizards concocted to shut Shaia up."

I was looking directly at him. He knew I was there, listening.

He knew.

I stared at him, wondering what I was.

Mistress Phae shook her head with a sound of disgust and shut the birthing room door on us both.

I was not invited to see the real child.

"Is she still my sister?" I asked.

Lord Ronar didn't answer me. He walked away to share the news of his daughter's birth.

That moment was only the first of many where I realized.

I no longer belonged.

I slept at the hearth in the kitchens that night. No one missed me or cried out an alarm. The cook shooed me out at dawn, screaming at me not to return.

Sometime that day Lord Ceolwyn found out what had happened. There were discussions. There were arguments. Being so young, I was not privy to any of them. I had no say in what would become of me.

The resolution was nearly as cruel as the event.

"I love you," my mother said as she held me close and

kissed the top of my head. "You are my son, and I will always love you, but I have to leave you here. You belong to the wizard now, and this will continue to be your home."

"What about you? Will you stay here, too?"

"We're leaving you here. Be strong, and be brave. You'll be safer without us."

I cried. I didn't understand. I couldn't understand. Being four, nearly five, I knew other kids my age who had big brothers and sisters, or little brothers and sisters. They had families. Even with brothers and sisters, they had families.

I had nothing.

It wasn't fair.

That was the last time I saw or even heard from Lord and Lady Ronar.

Lord Ceolwyn sighed and put a hand on my shoulder as we watched them ride away. "I'm not sure what I'm going to do with you," he said, "but you'll be better off here than with them. Humans can be so petty and short-sighted."

"You're not human?" I asked in wonder.

"As human as you are," he said with just a bit of a smile. "My mother was human. My father is an elf."

"Do I have a father?"

Lord Ceolwyn looked me over thoughtfully. "You're an experiment one of my colleagues worked on for a very long time. I know that it had something to do with a water spirit, so in a way, perhaps, the magical essence of water is your father."

I furrowed my brow. "Another wizard stuck a mint spear in my mom, and it had water all over it, and then I was born?"

"No. Not a spear of mint. An experiment. He was trying a new kind of magic to do something that had never been done before. That's how you were born."

"Oh," I said. I still didn't understand, but I had at least realized it was something only wizards could do, and whatever it was had failed because I wasn't the son my parents had wanted.

"We'll give you a room and a tutor," Lord Ceolwyn said. "You won't have to worry about a thing."

I nodded, numb from all the things that had happened and how quickly everything had changed. I did everything I was told, at first. Then again, I did only what I was told. I sat still a lot, staring off in thought. I had a birthday and no one noticed. I felt sorry for myself, and I was absorbed in that for a time, but it didn't last.

For one thing, life went on around me despite the pain.

For another, I was five years old and I was bored.

I was lonely.

More than anything, though, I was angry.

Every pure-blooded human I saw reminded me that humans were stupid, and they were wrong, and in the end they'd all go away. I wanted to make them all go away. I hated their faces and their ugly brown hairs and their flat ugly eyes in their ugly colors. Humans all looked too brown to me now, and I hated brown more than any other color. My hair was blue, Lord Ceolwyn's hair was silvery white, and those were the colors of his country. Silver and blue. His eyes were bright green and mine were as blue as my hair. I became nearly obsessed with color, to the point that I began painting the walls and adding dye to the food if I could sneak into the kitchens.

That was just the beginning of the pranks. Some of them I got caught at, and some of them I got away with. Punishment just gave me motivation to try harder to not get caught. Anything I did could be fixed with a bit of magic, and after a while punishment included magic lessons so that I could fix things myself.

That idea may have backfired on the grownups a bit. I started getting caught just so I could learn some new spell. I tailored my pranks to learn a spell that grabbed my attention. I never thought that this might be what they were trying to do. I was laughing too much at how stupid all these adults must be.

It went on for years. I grew up to be a troublemaker, and Lord Ceolwyn let me get away with it most of the time. Once in a while he took me aside himself to give me a lecture when I went too far. Only once, when something went very wrong, did he actually lose his temper at something I'd done. I'd been dangling on a rope from a casement to hide a book my tutor had been reading earlier that day, and the knot I'd tied had slipped loose. I'd fallen, and Lord Ceolwyn saved my life.

"You could have died!"

"So?" I didn't say it with any emotion except maybe mild curiosity. I'd had no idea it would actually matter.

"Be upset about that! Be afraid!" Lord Ceolwyn slammed his hand onto a nearby table in anger.

I remember it had been solid oak. It was a table I'd climbed on, run into, and used all the time. Several bruises I'd acquired over the years attested to how solid the table had been.

It exploded into a puff of ash.

"Be alive, Ysili! I thought you were enjoying yourself. Why don't you care if you live or die?"

For the first time since my sister was born, I was scared.

The idea of death didn't seem real or important, but the thought of a wizard being angry terrified me. I wanted to run but my feet wouldn't listen to me.

"Damn it," he swore under his breath. He grabbed my shoulders with almost bruising force and locked eyes with me, mere inches from my face. "You're important around here."

All I could do was stare. Did Lord Ceolwyn care? About me? Why?

His expression softened, and his hands upon me gentled. "If you won't believe I care for you, then believe this. There's something I need you to do. Not yet, but someday," he explained, brushing hair out of my eyes. No one had ever looked at me with as much kindness as he did at that moment. "There's a boy I'm looking for. He's been kidnapped, and I have no idea what he's been taught or what he will do when we find him. He will need a friend. Someone he can laugh with. Someone he can talk to and confide in. I need to take him away from his parents, and he'll need a friend who knows what that's like. I need you."

"Okay," I said in a small voice. "I'll try not to die."

Lord Ceolwyn sighed in relief. "Thank you." He held me close for a moment, like I was actually precious to him. "Thank you."

I didn't even know what he meant. I didn't know if that meant he cared, or if it meant he just needed me to do something for him and as soon as I was done he wouldn't need me anymore. Maybe when I was finished, maybe then it would be okay to die.

Eventually I learned more about the boy that Lord Ceolwyn wanted me to befriend. Immediately, I was disappointed to learn that he was human.

I'll admit, I was more intrigued than I was disappointed.

One of the first things I learned was that he was an elemental. That meant he was equal in all ways to a wizard, except that he was born with the powers of a god instead of stealing it from the gods themselves. He was supposed to be the lord of the country of Verwyn, which wasn't far from Ceolwyn.

"Do I have to call him Lord Verwyn when we're friends?"

Lord Ceolwyn smiled, shaking his head. "No. He probably doesn't know he's a wizard yet. He won't know what you're talking about. When you meet him, you can ask what he'd like to be called."

"And he'll ask me? Then we'll be friends?"

"That's the idea."

"Tell me more about him." If he was to be my purpose, my reason to live, I had to know everything.

"We don't know very much," he said. "We don't even know his name yet. His parents are Torba and Fadal Leyfraiin, and they used to be spellsmiths in my employ. They were very talented, and I'm afraid I taught them all they needed to know to stay hidden."

"Wouldn't he be Lord Leyfraiin?"

"That's not how it works," Lord Ceolwyn smiled at me patiently. "It's for the same reason that I'm not Lord Alavraneth. Wizards put everything behind us so that we can be the best wizards we can be, and concentrate on the countries we rule. We give up our family names and use the country names to remind us of where our greatest loyalty must be."

"I didn't know you had another name," I said, eyes wide.

"Focus," Lord Ceolwyn said. "I'm trying to tell you about Verwyn, not me. He has lived many, many lives but he won't remember any of them. Still, throughout them all, he's been clever, wise, and usually kind."

"Did you know him the last time he was alive?"

"I've known him every time he's been alive."

"Wow." I wasn't sure what to think of that. "Wouldn't you have to be really old to know him that many times?"

"I am very old," he chuckled. "Being a wizard means I can live as long as I want to, as long as no one kills me." Lord Ceolwyn cocked his head to the side with a bit of a frown. "Before you ask, yes. That means Verwyn has been killed many times. There have been wars, and he's always been there to fight in them." Sadness had crept into his eyes as he spoke, but he suddenly dismissed it with a shake of his head. "That's in the past. I called you in here because there's been news. I may be close to finding him, so you might get a chance to meet him soon. If so, would you like to come with me?"

I thought about it for a moment, but — "No, I'll stay here and make sure he has a room he'll like, and I'll pick out all the best toys." I liked the idea of traveling and meeting Verwyn, but more than that I liked the idea of the pranks I could pull without a wizard in the castle to lecture me again.

"Hmmm," he replied, looking at me with a sparkle in his eye that told me he was not fooled. "Very well. Make certain that the toys truly are the best, or else." He gave me a wink. "And don't do anything too dangerous or messy. I'd hate for you to be in the middle of a punishment when I return."

When he left I stayed behind, as agreed, excitement growing that I would finally have a friend. I daydreamed constantly of meeting him and teaching him all the tricks and hiding spots in the castle. We would learn all the same things, and play all the same games, and we wouldn't need anyone else but each other.

Things didn't go that way, though. It's something I've learned in life. Once things start going well, that's when it's time to worry.

Things don't go right when I most want them to.

Lord Ceolwyn returned suddenly in the middle of the night, injured and angry. I heard screaming and the sound of many people rushing to his aid. I crept from my room and hid in a corner to watch what was going on.

"You found him?"

Healers were coming in and out, and my tutor was at his side, listening and asking questions.

"His name is Agrad," Lord Ceolwyn said. "Write it down. He vanished, but I know him now. I'll find him. Send out word that I'm looking for him. Black hair. Light brown eyes. Olive skin, though mostly light from spending time indoors. That might change now. Nine, almost ten years old. Very pretty, in fact I almost mistook him for a girl. He's clever, and he's dangerous. Don't tell anyone he's dangerous, though. Just send out the word that he's an orphan, and I want to make sure he's safe and taken care of."

I stepped closer, careful not to get in the way. I saw now that Lord Ceolwyn was burned very badly, and they were slathering him with some sort of goop all over, from top to bottom. He was lying on his back, staring up at the ceiling. Injured and at the mercy of others, he suddenly looked small to me. I'd known that as a half-elf he was shorter than most humans, but he'd never seemed small before. It was a thought that disturbed me.

"Lord Ceolwyn," I said softly, "are you okay?"

He turned his head to look at me, wincing a bit from the pain of it. "You should be asleep, Ysili," he admonished gently. "I'm a wizard, I'll be fine. The blisters will be gone by the morning, and this will all be as if it were just a bad dream."

"What about Master Thenivstral and Mistress Kerb? Will they be okay, too?"

Lord Ceolwyn looked incredibly sad. "Go to bed. You need your sleep. You shouldn't be seeing this."

I nodded and I left. I realized that it must have been the worst fire in the world to burn Lord Ceolwyn so badly. Who but a wizard would have survived that? I went to bed, but I couldn't sleep. I thought of Agrad Verwyn and I wondered what had gone wrong. Was he burned and alone somewhere? Would I ever meet him? Would I ever be his friend?

The next two years were frantic. I traveled with Lord Ceolwyn whenever he heard a rumor of where Agrad might be. I saw more of the world in those years than I'd imagined had even existed. We visited large cities, like Plath and Urdran, and each of them were so very different from

Anogrin and from each other. We visited smaller towns like Stonegore and Lanrinborough and even a town on the edge of a cliff that boasted a total of seven families all told. I think the town's name was Blight, and the child they'd found was actually a southern elf child of fifty years. He'd gotten lost, but no one there knew the elf language. Lord Ceolwyn was able to help, but we were all frustrated with yet another false lead.

"I don't know how he's evading me," Lord Ceolwyn said, staring out the carriage window in obvious frustration. "His parents are dead. He said he wasn't allowed to use simple animation magic to turn rocks into toys, so I'm certain they never taught him how to hide himself. What am I missing?"

I didn't know how to answer him. "Maybe he just figured it out."

"I hope not," Lord Ceolwyn said, a line forming between his brows as his frown deepened. "He needs to be taught to control his powers before he hurts anyone else."

The words were a terrifying reminder of the night Lord Ceolwyn had returned with all those burns. It had been a disaster beyond what I'd imagined. The entire town had been wiped out in a fiery blast of raw magic, and only the two of them had survived. "You can teach him to be safe, though. Right?"

Lord Ceolwyn shook his head. "I doubt he'd ever trust me again. Someone else will have to do it."

"But how can I be his friend if he goes somewhere else?"

He patted my shoulder in assurance. "You'll go with him. Don't worry."

I nodded, but I wasn't entirely reassured. I'd never lived anywhere but Anogrin. The idea had always been that Agrad would join me, and I'd show him around and make him feel at home. It was a lot to fret over, but I wanted Lord Ceolwyn to be proud of me.

Eventually, the news came from Verwyn's own lands that another elemental had spotted Agrad by chance.

"Modarian Lorwyn is just one generation removed from being a wizard like me," Lord Ceolwyn explained to me as we traveled. "He remembers the days when we had to find young wizards, before we began training them from birth. I trust his assessment that this must be Agrad."

"Why didn't he just grab Agrad, then?" Silly waste of time, I thought to myself.

Lord Ceolwyn sighed. "Because he is smarter than I am, apparently." He waved a parchment around, and I assumed it was the correspondence between himself and Lord Lorwyn. "Or lazier. He's never been particularly open with his motives."

I didn't know what to say to that, and we lapsed into silence.

I'm stalling in my story now. How I got along with Krecek Ceolwyn, all the fears and false starts of my childhood are mere distractions to what I need to actually put into words. It's harder to write about than I'd expected, but it's time.

The real story begins with betrayal.

We knew Agrad was on the road, running from us. A lady he'd spent a night with had turned him in for the reward, and Lord Ceolwyn was happy to give it, and more, to her and her family. She acted ashamed of herself and nearly refused the reward, but she looked at the little boy clinging to her skirt and nodded with a hand outstretched. I shoved down a stab of envy at seeing that glance and the knowledge that she was sacrificing her morals for the sake of her child. It was none of my business.

Only one thing mattered.

We were close.

We left her small cottage and set up a pavilion in a small clearing down the road a bit. I watched Lord Ceolwyn cast magic that, for the first time, made me realize the scope of what a wizard's power might be. A storm roiled out from where we stood as he softly murmured words beyond any magic I'd heard before. The clouds reached from horizon to horizon, and he almost absently controlled every raindrop and lightning bolt.

Awe-inspiring doesn't begin to cover it.

It didn't feel magical, it was just like a natural storm from all I could tell with my well-honed magic sense. If I hadn't seen him create it, I might have been fooled. Within his hands he held a clear sphere, something between a soap bubble and a crystal ball, and it showed the whole of the storm, and every spell cast beneath the dark canopy left a momentary red spark.

He used it to track Agrad to a cave near the Mirren River. Over the course of a few days a handful of other wizards joined us. I wasn't introduced to any of them, I was simply there, like a tent pole or a cot. They spent their time talking over what to do, helping narrow down exactly where he was, and a great debate ensued among them.

"It was Verwyn magic," I heard someone say, "it's pretty

clear, isn't it?"

This made me look up from the book I'd been reading. Lord Ceolwyn was nodding, staring at a spot that was a different shade of red that lingered longer than most flashes of spells in the bauble he held. He looked up and met my gaze.

"Ysili," he said with an added unspoken command to join him.

As I set aside my book he turned to the others and explained who I was and why I was there.

"He'll keep an eye on Verwyn, befriend the boy and keep him in check. I've been training Ysili in how to do this for many years."

I stood tall and proud, happy to finally be acknowledged by those assembled. I was ready to fulfill my purpose in life at last.

"How will Verwyn react, though?" The wizard who spoke was a lady with bushy, dark brown hair and oddly flat black eyes that seemed to absorb light. "He's already proven skittish, and he has no love of us or reason to trust this blue-haired child."

"We could play on his sympathies," another wizard, a tall man, mused. "Verwyn has, traditionally at least, been a caring and protective sort. It's part of his innate nature, written in his soul. He's someone who couldn't walk away from someone injured or in pain."

I looked at Lord Ceolwyn, confused, and saw the life drain from his expression. The color in his cheeks, the twinkle in his eyes, retreated in an instant.

The tall human began speaking again, but as I looked in his direction all I saw was a bow in his hand and an arrow ready to be nocked.

I started to back away, knowing immediately where this would end.

"That's right. Pretend to be running away from us."

"Stop!" Lord Ceolwyn put his hand on the tall wizard's arm, and for a moment I thought he had a better idea. That I would be saved from whatever pain the other wizard wanted to put me through. But I was wrong. "He's in my care. Ysili is my ward. I'll do this myself."

That's when I ran.

I won't describe what it felt like. I don't want to. It was painful, of course. It was also surreal. I made it to the cave somehow. I snapped the arrow in two with a magic blow that left me dizzy and panting. A fire sprang to life beside me, and a pack appeared next to me with a few necessities. I didn't even think about where they came from.

In a haze of pain I dressed the wound myself and poured whatever alcohol Lord Ceolwyn had provided over the opening. It felt like I'd poured fire through my leg. I remember taking a drink and feeling a fire in my throat to rival that of my leg, but I didn't care because I knew the drink would dull the throbbing pain. I remember trying to use strips of my shirt as a bandage, and my fingers wouldn't obey like I thought they should.

My ass was suddenly hit by the ground as a dark haze crept in on my vision. I felt the cool caress of stone rubbing against my face as the darkness completely claimed me.

Interlude One

Ysili jumped, startled by the sound of a knock at the door.

"Not right now! I'm busy!"

He shoved the pages into a drawer anyway, just in case someone barged in despite his demand.

"Dinner is nearly ready."

The door didn't swing open. He heard soft footfalls pad away from the door and down the hallway, leaving him alone with his mess of words and memories.

"What am I doing?" he asked the empty room. "Nobody cares how it all started. I'm a nothing and my past doesn't matter to anyone."

Ysili stared balefully at the drawer, tempted for a moment to burn the pages he'd already written. It was just a bunch of self-loathing put into words after all. But, there was something cathartic about going through it all again, writing it down. The loathing he had for his parents, the fear he still fought down every time he looked upon the face of a wizard or elemental, Lord Ceolwyn most of all.

Maybe someone would care at some point in the future. Maybe his words would be part of history.

Or maybe he'd burn it all once he was done, and grin that his past was finally behind him.

Yes. Burn it all.

But get it all down on paper, first. If for nothing else, maybe it would give him peace of mind at last.

He locked the drawer and put the key in its cubby hole. Something within him felt lighter as he stood. Was it the burden of his childhood being lifted from his shoulders? Or was it the promise of food?

Probably the food, he decided as he headed out the door.

II – Agrad

The moment I laid eyes on Agrad Verwyn I both loathed and admired him in equal measure. He looked so plainly human, with his brown eyes, his lightly tan skin, his black hair. He blended into the stone and shadow of the cave, except for the colors of the girl's dress he was wearing. The dress was white with pale blue flowers dyed into it, and it contrasted against his body in a strikingly beautiful manner.

But it was him, he said his name was Agrad, and he began helping me immediately. He had the delicate features and graceful motions of a girl, and for a moment I thought the wizards had sent me here by mistake, or that I'd been found by someone else coincidentally named Agrad.

A book I'd once read sprang to mind, about messengers of the gods, called angels.

I was giddy from pain, and potential triumph, when he offered all his bandages and ointment. As soon as I thought of that book the words came out. "Are you an angel," I laughed, "or am I just lucky?"

If angels were real, and still around, maybe they'd help an enemy of the gods? Since a wizard had shot me with an arrow, would such a creature save me?

No. It was a foolish thought. An angel would know I'd spent my life among wizards.

This was a human child.

A human child with the power of a god.

Agrad looked guilty, and afraid. "An angel would have healed you by now." He poked at the fire, downcast as he apologized.

I grimaced. "An angel would have shot me a second time, to make sure," I said. I was a creature of wizards. I'd thought of myself as Lord Ceolwyn's friend, and now I was trying to befriend another wizard. A servant of the gods would have killed me, and the thought made me laugh. "I'll take my chances with ordinary folk, thanks."

"I'm ordinary?"

And of course, he wasn't.

He knew it, too, by the look he gave me.

The giddiness continued, and now I wonder how much of it was pain and blood loss, and how much of it was coming face to face with the only purpose I'd ever been given. I hadn't yet thought about betraying Lord Ceolwyn's directives, despite what he had done. I hadn't had time to process what had happened, and my loyalty was automatic. Meeting Agrad, being shot by the only person I'd trusted, it all felt surreal and when I woke up, I half expected it all to have been a dream.

I healed eventually, using what magic I had learned. It was limited, and at times I grew frustrated that I wasn't at home where a healer would have mended the wound easily in no time. I'd broken my leg, an ankle, and even my arm once in my reckless explorations. Lord Ceolwyn had healed me at times, like white fire searing my bones together. Other times, when he was away, the healers would gently and slowly mend the bones over days. I wish I could have summoned that white fire. I'd have welcomed the pain for the freedom I knew that would follow.

Agrad was afraid of the rain. Afraid to be caught. I'd tried to push the matter a few times, tried to let him know it was fine to do magic now without telling him that I knew who he was. Our lies danced around each other, never meeting, never offering a satisfying resolution. He snapped at me a few times, saying he couldn't, or wouldn't, heal me. I had to let it go. Getting a wizard angry at me, even an untrained one, didn't seem like the smartest thing I could do with my life.

But, some perverse, self-destructive part of me couldn't help but needle him despite knowing I should be cautious.

"I love the way you wait on me hand and foot," I said at one point, grinning. "It's like having a servant. I've always wanted to have one, rather than being one."

"I'm not your servant," Agrad muttered, thrusting the water skin into my hands roughly.

"You act like one," I pointed out. "It's almost as good. Where I came from, I'd have to fetch things for others all the time, if I stood still long enough to let someone notice me. The trick is to always look busy with something more important than fetching things. I suppose it's hard to look too busy here, though. Can you fetch me a peach? I ate the last one while you were out."

He looked outside, chewing his bottom lip thoughtfully.

"If there aren't any good peaches, some more cherries would do, so long as there are enough of them. Take your time. If you bring me back just one or two, that's not even worth the effort, now is it?"

He shook his head. "Can you teach me to heal?"

I suddenly understood why he'd been looking outside. The sky was clear. The storm that Lord Ceolwyn had summoned was gone, and all traces of the spell had faded.

Agrad thought he was safe.

I'd fooled him. He didn't suspect that I was a spy. It had worked.

"Oh good," I said, grinning. "Then I can go get whatever I want out there. I'll bet you've been holding out on me and you're more powerful than you let on."

He shook his head and wouldn't meet my eyes. "I'll get you a peach first. But, when I come back. Teach me." He practically ran from the cave before I could answer.

Upon his return I taught him the spell, and he picked it up immediately. I'd never met someone who learned magic so fast. When he set his hands on my leg and began the spell I expected him to be as quick, as powerful, and as painful as Lord Ceolwyn had been. I prepared myself, holding my breath, but the pain never came.

I didn't understand at first. Yet again I found myself doubting that I'd found the right person. How many people, his age, named Agrad, were out hiding in the woods? Had I wasted all this time, all this pain, on the wrong Agrad?

It couldn't be. I could feel how powerful he was. I could feel magic in the air around him. I knew from all my time around Lord Ceolwyn, and even from meeting other wizards, that it felt like Agrad was a wizard. He had to be Verwyn. He had to be. So, why wouldn't he heal me?

He must still be afraid, I realized.

I mean, of course he was. Why wouldn't he be? The spell was gone, but he'd been on the run long before the storm. Clear skies didn't mean he was safe. It was a healthy skepticism to have... and I was proof of that, even if he didn't know it.

Later we were talking about what we'd do when we got to the city, and his eyes darted around, looking for someone who wasn't there to jump out at him, to capture him.

"You'd make more if you apprenticed to a mage or a spellsmith," I'd tried to point out. "Scribes are rare, but—"

"No magic."

His eyes were narrowed, and his eyebrows were trying to merge into one long line at his brow. It wasn't any sort of self-doubt that fueled his protest. The words were a firm statement. Damn it. This was going to make things harder than it should be. The plan was to guide him to the city safely, set him up in a cushy position befitting his station, and be his friend. Simple, right?

What sort of a position could a child without magic do that wasn't dangerous, grueling, backbreaking work? How fast would he be forced to abandon his disguise if there was an accident? Or a conspicuous lack of accidents?

I was going to fail at this, and it wasn't even my fault.

"We'll think of something," I said, thinking of Lord Ceolwyn. He'd be disappointed in me, but he'd tell me what to do next when I saw him again. If I saw him again. I had a thought then, a small idea... "I just don't want to attract too much attention, you know?"

If we didn't attract attention, maybe I could hide from Lord Ceolwyn with Agrad. He could hide me and protect me the way he'd hidden himself this long.

Call me crazy, but I wasn't sure I wanted to keep working for someone who shot me in the leg.

"Me too," Agrad said, voice soft. He looked at me, eyes piercing straight into my soul. "Is that how you got shot?"

I froze. Do wizards read minds? Did Agrad know what I was thinking? No, he couldn't, or he wouldn't be asking.

He'd have left me to die if he could read my mind.

Would Lord Ceolwyn have come to save me, if Agrad hadn't taken the bait?

I held Agrad's gaze, took a shallow breath, and refused to answer. I asked, instead, "Is that why you won't use magic?" I felt smug turning the tables on him.

I knew he wouldn't answer me. He never answered direct questions like that, he thought he had too much to hide.

But his eyes still bored into mine.

"Yes."

It was simple, it was honest, and it was nothing I didn't know. Useless.

Still, I smiled as he walked away. His honesty showed a glimmer of trust. It's what I was sent here to gain.

Maybe, just maybe, I'd succeed after all.

Mornings grew colder as we traveled, which brought dew and frost to the grass in the morning, which added to the slippery muck and mud as the day went on. The ruts in the road accumulated the worst of it, but the edges could be deceptively slick. That's what caught Agrad one afternoon, sliding him fully into a puddle of mud.

A kind local girl invited us inside her estate, and I was immediately wary and on edge. With all the trappings of wealth, and the proximity to Cairnborough, this couldn't be a chance encounter. My suspicions were confirmed as soon as Agrad was in the bath.

"You're a filthy liar, Ysili Ronar," the girl said with a sweet smile on her face, still looking at the door Agrad had disappeared behind.

I spread my hands wide, admitting my guilt without apology. "You enjoyed the story, and you've told a bit of a tale, yourself. Who are you, really?"

"Visandra Cerine," she said self-importantly, as if I should recognize her name. When I didn't give her the reaction she expected she huffed and went on. "Lord Lorwyn told me the two of you would be here eventually, and I've been waiting for days."

"We've been walking," I said. "So sorry to keep your ladyship waiting."

"No need to be snide about it." Visandra looked me over, then her expression settled on a half grin. "So, is that really him? He really does look like a girl."

"It had better be him," I grumbled. "He fits the description and has the right name. He's got the same feel a wizard does."

"Feel?" Her expression turned quizzical, then she laughed. "Oh! You mean magic. For a moment I thought you meant their skin is bumpy or scaly or something."

I wasn't laughing. "You know what I mean, though," I persisted.

"No." She shrugged it off, but her eyes had narrowed just a bit. "I don't do magic. You know most people can't. Right?"

"Oh, well, of course I knew that," I lied. No one had ever

told me that, I'd assumed that casting spells and sensing magic was normal. But I couldn't admit my ignorance to this know-it-all girl. "I've just spent so much time in Anogrin that it's rare to meet someone who can't."

"They're not more magical there," she said, then pursed her lips a moment before going on. "It's not as if having a bit of magic makes you better than me. You work for a wizard, the same as the rest of us. I don't feel like I'm missing anything, since I can get whatever I want by asking. I'm a direct descendant of Garm Lorwyn, after all."

"Oh." That explained why she thought I'd recognize her name at least. I hadn't bothered really learning much about the original wizards. They were names and dates that didn't mean much other than they were people that Lord Ceolwyn used to know. "That must be nice."

Visandra leaned forward, brows knit together. "Well, you're a member of the Ronar family. Daichen Eudwyn was born with the name Ronar, and he–"

"It's just a name," I cut her off, irritated. My parents were diplomats. My parents were a lord and lady. I was a nothing. I was discarded. "Do you know what I got for asking for things? I got left behind. I got shot in the leg with an arrow. I get to walk from the middle of nowhere to Cairnborough with a kid who barely tolerates my presence, and I have to be his best friend no matter what."

"What?" She looked startled, concerned. "What do you mean, shot in the leg? Where are your parents? Why didn't they stop this?"

"They left." I stared her down, not saying another word, until she bowed her head. "You're a lady, I'm a nothing. I do magic because maybe, if I'm lucky, I'll be good enough to be useful after Agrad is dealt with."

"So, you don't look down on me for not having magic?"

The almost silent question stabbed through me like a blade in the night. After a moment I realized my mouth was hanging open and I shut it with abrupt irritation at myself. What sort of fool was I to show my surprise?

"I don't know you well enough to look down on you," I said. I didn't trust this sudden vulnerability from her. Was this human trying to gain my sympathy? This puffed-up princess of a girl?

She looked up at me and smiled, and I didn't like that smile. That genuine, honest, hopeful smile that said something was broken inside, and I'd inadvertently been kinder to her than I'd wanted to be. A smile that said she liked what I'd said, despite my irritation. Or, perhaps, because of it. Of course, I didn't think it through so thoroughly at the time. I just registered my own discomfort. It's a smile that stayed with me and made me wonder what was behind it years after it was gone.

Were her parents as disappointed in her for how she was born as mine had been in me? If I'd never had a little sister, would I have the same sort of life as this girl? I didn't like any part of that thought, wanted nothing to do with it, but there it sat before me.

"It doesn't make us friends, just because your lack of magic doesn't bother me."

"Of course not."

Visandra was still giving me the same smile.

"We'll be gone as soon as possible, and you'll never hear from us again."

Visandra shook her head. "I travel through Cairnborough

to the summer estate here twice a year. We may run into each other again. It would be nice to have someone to look forward to seeing."

I didn't have an answer to that. How long would we actually be in Cairnborough? "Maybe."

"We might see each other in Anogrin, once we're all grown up."

"We might not be able to stand the look of each other's faces by then."

"Or we might like them better."

I scowled. "Agrad might get jealous." I'd given her a story about how Agrad and I were betrothed and had run away together in face of the betrothal being called off, or some nonsense like that. Visandra had eaten it up and acted like a hopeless romantic over it, and apparently that was less an act and more her personality.

"I hate to think of what a jealous wizard would be like." She giggled and leaned toward me. "I don't think he would be, though. He's a boy and you're a boy."

"He's a boy that's acting like a girl. It might make him different." He might turn out like some of the men who had fawned over Lord Ceolwyn. They'd had as much chance of joining the wizard at night as women had, which was rare on both counts as far as I was aware. Still, it was no secret, and no shame, that for some the gender of one's partners didn't matter in the least, and I was still trying to figure out which side of that particular fence I might end up on myself.

The way she'd said that, as if mocking the idea of a boy being jealous about another boy, was all the warning I needed that she didn't share the same ideas I'd been raised with. What if that was the way of the rest of the world, outside the walls

84

I'd been raised in? What if Agrad had been raised to think that trysts, or more, weren't acceptable between men because he'd been raised among common humans? I silently told myself to be careful and guard myself around him, if any feelings arose.

"It might," she admitted. "If it doesn't, perhaps we should arrange to meet once we're grown."

I doubted that would be a good idea.

She was just a human, after all.

III – Cairnborough

The contact's name I was given was Mela Relata. It was the sort of name that rolled off the tongue in a pleasant way, and I expected an equally pleasant woman to be matched with the name. Instead, her face was reminiscent of a potato, her body a broomstick, and her personality was akin to sandpaper for the soul. To top it off it took two days to find out where she was, and another day trying to convince a half-dwarf to introduce us in a way that Agrad wouldn't find suspicious.

"You're a hard woman to track down," I said as I took her measure.

"Everyone in the city knows who I am. I'm short on space and have a list of children ahead of you who need room and board." She moved to usher me out the door before.

"Lord Ceolwyn sent me to you, I need —"

"I don't answer to any wizard," she cut me off. "Cairnborough is neutral ground, and as far as Ceolwyn is concerned he can piss up a rope for all I care." Mela had stopped in her tracks though, and was looking at me through narrowed eyes. "Master Tennival, on the other hand, is an old family friend. He told me you'd be coming on the wizard's behalf. Didn't say anything about the blue hair."

"I don't think he knows what I look like, I've never met Lord Tennival."

"Not 'lord'," she corrected me. "Not around here. He's Master Tennival and calling him a lord brands you an outsider. Says he doesn't like to put on airs, and we all respect it. Well, deliver your message and be on your way. I'll tell him I saw you."

"I don't have a message," I snapped. "I have a person, and I have one coin left to survive on." I held out the silver wheel Agrad had handed me earlier. "I was supposed to have more, but apparently wizards forget that us mere mortals need food and shelter to survive, and that means coin. You were the only contact I was given, so if you don't have food or shelter, I'll have to go find the nearest wizard and protest, formally, at the treatment we've been given." I wanted to shout, but I somehow managed to keep my voice low enough not to draw the attention of every child caterwauling in the spacious hall.

"Can you get more coin than that?" she asked, one eye going a bit wider as she gazed at the coin.

"If I don't starve or freeze to death first."

"Regularly?"

I nodded.

"I suppose you have rich parents who are supposed to supply you with—"

"No." I just about growled the word out, anger overtaking me at the words. "No parents, and it's best not to mention. Agrad is an orphan and I'm—"

I stopped. I might as well be an orphan, but I wasn't. Not technically.

I cleared my throat and continued. "I might as well be."

Her expression softened a touch for just a moment, then she snatched the coin from my hand and handed me a key. "It's little more than a closet, and you'll have to work for it. This place doesn't run itself, and I've got bills to pay with the money I collect. It's food and fire and a roof over your head, which seems to be better than what the wizards had in mind for you. Well, call your friend over so I can tell you both the rules. I hate having to repeat myself."

I smiled over at Agrad and waved him over. It wasn't the success I'd hoped for, but we wouldn't die. Well, Agrad would have survived no matter what, being an elemental. So, I wouldn't die.

Not yet.

Cairnborough gave me freedom I hadn't experienced or expected before. I let Agrad and everyone else who lived under Mela Relata's roof assume I was up to nefarious deeds to make a coin, but in truth most of it came directly from Naran Tennival.

"I'm an old friend of Krecek's" he said with a wry twist to his lips when we finally met. "I've been expecting you and your companion, and it's good to see the two of you safe."

I nodded and looked him over. Master Tennival was about average human height, towering over me when we met, but that wouldn't last. There was confidence in his stance, and he was a picture of trim health without signs of overindulgence. His hair was almost golden, but in my mind that was just another shade of human brown. His eyes, though, were blue, and I could almost forgive him for it.

As a friend of Krecek Ceolwyn's, I couldn't trust him. I had to watch what I said and how I said it.

"It's an honor to meet you," I said, chafing under just the right amount of deference toward someone who spoke for the wizards. "We're safe for now, but we don't even have two nubs to rub together for warmth this winter. What do the wizards plan to do next, now that he's safe?"

"Well, aren't you the little soldier? Down to business, hmm? Very well." Master Tennival sat back with a thoughtful look. "I have been given a small amount of coin to pass along to you for your continued service in this matter. Entirely your money to do with as you please." He handed over a fistful of silver coins, a few wheels and a star. "As to Agrad himself, the wizards are divided on how to go forward. For now, we want to let him settle in and get comfortable so he's less likely to run and disappear again."

I nodded slowly, thinking. "Am I to stay here with him for as long as it takes?"

"Of course." Master Tennival smiled in a way that brought warmth to his ice blue eyes. "The two of you have become friends already, from what I understand. It would be a shame to tear the two of you apart."

"Okay." That was good, right?

After all, at this point where else would I go?

"I'll watch out for both of you. Don't worry."

What if I didn't want him to look out for me? Or, what if he meant he'd be keeping an eye on me to keep me in line?

I'd never escape.

Never.

"Thank you, Master Tennival. I appreciate your aid."

What else could I say to him? My fate was in this human's hands, like it or not.

"Alright, you. What's going on here?" Bledig had come up on my right side, and Paelloret on my left. "You're not one of us, even if you do have Agrad fooled."

"Doesn't seem too hard to do," Paelloret added. "She's pretty, but a bit oblivious."

Agrad and I had been in Cairnborough weeks, and I'd thought myself particularly clever in spending every moment alone simply walking around and learning every part of the city. Agrad didn't probe too deep into the idea that I'd become an ordinary pickpocket, despite my unique blue hair that would give me away to any passersby. I came home with unexplained coin, and that was enough for him.

"I don't know what you're talking about," I said, feeling a prickle at the back of my neck and a frisson of nervousness flow through me.

"You don't?" Bledig guffawed and met Paelloret's eyes. "Oh, well, we must be wrong about him, then. Ysili's obviously a thief like us, a common thug, right as rain and as normal as can be."

"Oh, of course," Paelloret agreed. "A very good one, being as there's been no word of mouth about a strange blue-haired boy getting caught or being seen at the scene of anything untoward. Impressive to have the whole of the network of us completely fooled."

"Network?"

Bledig shook his head. "You didn't even figure out that much?"

"Should I have?"

"If you want to survive here for long."

Spells I'd learned years ago for pranks sprang to mind immediately, and I took half a step back to get out from between the two. "Is that a threat?"

The two of them stopped when I did and turned to face me.

"Maybe. If it needs to be." Paelloret had a knife in his hand suddenly, accompanied by the tell-tale thrill of magic that told me he had conjured it rather than producing it from somewhere on his body.

We weren't far from Mistress Relata's haven, just around the corner in fact, still in the bad part of town. They'd steered me toward a small alleyway, and even my one step back wouldn't be enough to offer any real chance at escape if this got ugly.

"You're a mage?"

"I know a spell or two. I'm an elf, after all. It's not just pointy ears and keen senses; we were the favored of the gods."

That changed things a bit. "A spell or two" could be simple conjuration and maybe something ridiculous like repelling insects. Or it could be something dangerous, like being able to shut off someone's airway with nothing but a thought. I could defend myself, but I wasn't a wizard or a mage. I couldn't cast spells silently or instantly, the way

Paelloret had with his conjuring, and that put me at a disadvantage.

"So, what do you want from me?" I was playing a desperate mental game of figuring out which of the spells I knew could defend me against a complete unknown. Unfortunately, worry was making that almost impossible.

Bledig frowned. "Answers. Well, one answer. If you're not one of us, why are you pretending to be?"

I wanted to be able to tell them the truth. The truth would be easier to keep track of, and I was itching to be able to tell someone, anyone, what I was involved in. On top of it, neither of them was fully human, Bledig having dwarven ancestry and Paelloret being a full-blooded elf. It made me inclined to trust them.

"Look, we're hiding from wizards," I said, which would at least be in keeping with what Agrad thought was the truth. "We're just trying to keep a low profile and survive. I don't know the first thing about stealing, but Agrad will worry if I'm doing something that seems too risky. A proper apprenticeship might get me caught, because I have an aptitude for magic. If she knew I had actual employment she would worry and might insist we run away again. I'm tired of running. But if I got caught picking a pocket or so much as snatching bread from a cart, well, you have eyes. If anything is pinned on a boy with blue hair, I won't be hard to single out. So, I've been taking odd jobs, mostly running messages and small items between clients."

"You picked a bad city to hide from wizards," Paelloret said softly. The knife was gone, and he gestured me toward a couple of barrels and boxes sitting nearby. "They've all got ties here, and they visit now and again."

91

"Actually, this might be the best place." Bledig had a big grin on his face as he sat down. "The audacity of hiding under their noses has a certain appeal, and it's not a small town. There's a lot of people in this city and hiding in plain sight just might work."

"I hope so," I lied. "In smaller towns we stood out more, and as outsiders no one was really willing to help." Another lie. "I might look unique, but it's Agrad the wizards really want, and I doubt they're even really looking for me, just her." A bit of bait to see what they'd do with the knowledge that Agrad was wanted.

"Your secrets are safe with us," Bledig said solemnly. "So long as our secrets are safe with you. We don't want their attention on us any more than you'd want it on you."

It was probably as much a threat as it was an agreement. Bledig had been helping me since we met, showing me around. He'd shown me how to find Mistress Relata. But we weren't yet fast friends who had earned any sort of loyalty from each other.

The air was cold enough that our breaths were coming in little puffs, uncomfortable but not yet dangerous. It was just a reminder of weather to come, and it gave me an idea. "Paelloret, before I lost my home, I'd been taught some magic, too. I could teach you a spell if you'd like." He nodded, and I carefully enunciated a few words of magic and held out my hands to show the exact gestures necessary to a warmth spell. The magic energy coalesced into a hazy red sphere before me and emanated just enough heat to warm my hands with when I grasped it. I then handed it to the elf child with as genuine a smile as I could muster. "It lasts a few hours, and you can slip it into a pocket to hide it from others."

It was the best peace offering I had, considering winter was on our doorstep.

Paelloret examined the orb, put it in his pocket when prompted, and tried to mimic the motions I'd made. "You'll teach me the whole spell?"

My peace offering was accepted. I relaxed and sat down, finally, to teach, to talk, and to make the first real steps of making new friends. Well, as close to friends as I could afford to make under the circumstances.

"How was your day?" Agrad asked softly. "Is everything okay?"

I sat down heavily and sighed. "Sure. It's just been a long day." I reached down and tugged off my boots, wiggling my toes at the sudden freedom. These were boots I'd been given for Dawnsday, and I'd had plenty of room to let my feet grow into them, but now they were cramped and wearing thin. Nightwatch was coming and I'd been running messages in three snowstorms with these boots trying to crowd out both my winter socks and my very feet.

"I have money," he said. "I've got a job. I'll be a model for an artist, a Master Tennival. We ran into each other on the street a few days ago, and today he offered me a job."

To prove it he dropped a silver wheel on the dresser and gave me a lopsided grin.

"I'm sorry I was so grumpy earlier," he went on. "Take this, use it on whatever you want."

"What?" I thought I was supposed to be supporting us

both with what Master Tennival gave me. It was tight, but I was confident I could do it. We'd be fine, we'd be safe....

"Pay our rent, get yourself necessities, new boots, whatever you want. It's the least I could do for you, for putting up with me. I've been useless since we got here, and I'd have been completely lost without you. Probably would have starved or frozen to death by now."

No. He would have resorted to using magic. He probably thought that would lead to being caught, tortured, or put to death, but it would take more than hunger and cold to kill a wizard or elemental. I nodded anyway, agreeing at least that the situation could have been desperate.

"I really appreciate your help, and your friendship. You could have left me behind at any time, once your leg was healed, but you didn't."

"You watched over me while I was hurt," I said, forcing a smile. I felt so fake. I didn't have a choice, I had to be his loyal friend. "It's the least I could do."

"You've paid that back many times over." His smile was brilliant, and innocent, like the girl he pretended to be. My heart didn't know there was a difference and skipped a beat with the force of that smile. "Will you stay with me still, now that we're both bringing in enough coin to survive?"

"Yes."

He hugged me tight. "Thank you. You're my best friend, you know."

All I could do was nod and hug him back. This wouldn't last forever. When he found out I had been ordered about and hired to watch him by the very people he was trying to hide from, would he forgive me? Would he explode and destroy everything like he'd done to his hometown? Would he absently erase me from existence for betraying him?

My only chance, my only hope, was that he might never find out.

IV – Lies and Liars

"Why did you decide to go by your real name here?"

Agrad looked up from the book he'd borrowed from Master Tennival, brow furrowed. "Do you think I shouldn't have?"

It was a moot point, even if he didn't realize it. We all knew who he was, where he was, and how to find him at any moment. He didn't know that, but it tickled my curiosity anyway.

"I'm just curious," I said. "You introduced yourself as Agrad to me when we met, but most of the time we were traveling you called yourself Eria. It's a pretty name."

Agrad carefully put the bookmark into the book, just under the line he'd been reading, and set it aside with meticulous care. "I could hide in small towns as Eria and be someone I'm not, or I could be one of hundreds of people named Agrad in a big city and be me. We met three women and five men named Agrad or some variant the first three days we were here."

"There was an elemental named Agret a long time ago," I said. It was one of many boring history lessons my tutor had given me, and I'd only remembered the name because it had sounded similar to Agrad. "I think she died in the third wizard war or something. Anyway, I think that's why the name got popular."

He tilted his head to one side, just looking at me intently for a moment before he nodded. "I guess she was popular and well liked," he said. "Maybe my mom named me after her, so I'd be well liked, too."

"Maybe." I got up from my cot and stretched. "It suits you. Where'd you come up with the name Eria, though?"

"The people who took me in," he said, and his voice was quiet as he spoke. "When my mom and dad died, I didn't talk. It was like, if I said anything, it would make it real that they were gone." He paused, looked at the book, then at me again. "They had to call me something, so they named me after their daughter. She was dead."

That sounded painful for both Agrad and the couple who took care of him, honestly. It was like being erased in a way. Being called by a different name, being unable to correct them because the pain of living with what had happened was just too big. It reminded me of when my parents left me behind, except everyone had already known my name. Everything else had changed, but I'd been left with a useless name given to me by useless humans.

"They were nice," Agrad went on, eyes distant. "They taught me a lot, and they didn't mind that I didn't talk. They said I was a gift, and they treated me like they meant it."

"So why did you leave?" I wouldn't have left a home where I was wanted.

"They were priests," he said, his eyes darting around the room as if checking for spies. "An outsider came to town, and I think he was a wizard. I got scared that they'd get caught, so

I ran away."

"A wizard?" I froze in mid-stretch and stared. "Which one?"

"I don't know," he said.

I knew, of course, but I had a part to play. Pretending to be alarmed, pretending to not know, had to be automatic so that Agrad wouldn't suspect the truth. It suddenly irritated me that I had to lie, that I had to pretend, that I couldn't just be myself with him. He kept secrets, I kept secrets, and it was all so stupid because real friends didn't lie to each other all the time. I'd never have a true friend again because of this, because I couldn't tell Paelloret, or Bledig, or even Tanyai who we really were or why we were here without risking it all getting back to Agrad, without risking him running away again.

Agrad winced and continued. "He might have just been a mage. I don't know much about wizards, maybe he was just really powerful or had a lot of protection spells on him." His tone was apologetic, growing more so by the moment. "He was in a black carriage, and he wore black and silver, that's all I know."

I thought I'd hidden my irritation well. I hadn't acted at all like how I felt, but he'd picked up on it anyway. A thrill of fear lanced through me.

"It was weeks before we met," he assured me immediately, clearly reacting to my fear. "I don't know who he was looking for, for sure, but it couldn't have been you. Or if it was, he wasn't anywhere near you, ever. You're safe."

No. I wasn't safe.

I picked up a fresh shirt and changed clothes in record time. "I need to go take care of something I just remembered,"

I said. "I'll be back tonight."

Agrad stood in my way, his ruffled skirt took up most of the doorway so there wasn't any easy way past. "We're safe here," he emphasized, going so far as to put a hand on my arm. "I'll keep you safe. I promise."

It took everything I had to calm my emotions and try to keep my mind a total blank. "Just thinking about the wizards makes me nervous. I'll feel better if I can have a look around and make sure there aren't any nearby."

"You'll warn me if you find any?"

I nodded. "If I can."

He took a step away from the door, and I almost bolted away.

"I don't think he knows he's doing it," I flailed my arms around in a gesture of helplessness, "but he's picking up on my emotions, reacting to how I feel even if I'm hiding it. I can't do this. I can't keep lying to him like this. It's going to get me killed!"

Master Tennival sat behind his desk, toying with a slip of paper that sat before him while I rambled on and on and told him what had just happened. He looked at me calmly, waited a few moments in the face of my sudden silence, then nodded. "You're sure he's actually acting on your emotions and not your body language?"

I scowled. "You've had me practicing in front of a mirror for months, teaching me what to do and what not to do and how to appear calm all the time. I didn't do anything wrong.

He just knows! He changes what he's saying at the drop of a hat based on just what I'm feeling."

"Ysili, you don't have to stay if you don't want to. If you think you're in danger, leave."

My jaw dropped. That was his answer?

"Go back to Krecek and remind him you're still just a child, remind him that what he's asked of you, and what he's done to you, isn't fair." He leaned forward, his expression was of pure and genuine concern. "None of us want you put in harm's way, Ysili. You've done so much already that none of us could have done. It would be fine to walk away and say you can't do what they're asking of you. You're not a wizard. You don't have to sacrifice your life for them."

"I don't want to quit!" I hadn't meant to shout the words, hadn't really meant to say them, but I blurted them out anyway. "I'm not useless, I'm not worthless, I can — "

"I'm not saying you are," Master Tennival said gently. "I'm saying that Krecek and the others are asking a lot of you. More than is fair."

"No, I can do this. Agrad is my friend, and I don't want to lose that when he finds out the truth. I just need help." I wanted to protect him and be there for him. The more I got to know him and his ridiculously fussy ways, the more I liked him. I never told Master Tennival, or anyone, but Agrad would have nightmares and I'd hold him close the rest of the night. He'd cling to me like I was the only person in the world, and it was killing me that I wasn't worthy of that trust. "Please. Maybe we could just tell him."

"I don't think we can," he said. "Not yet. He'd only run away again. The plan is to give him time to live a normal life, as normal as he can while he thinks he's managed to hide.

We'll give him time to heal, emotionally, before he has to contend with what it means to be a Verwyn."

"He'll need a lot of that." I sighed and looked down at the ornate and obviously expensive rug beneath me. "Will I get help?"

"I'll ask my sister if she can spare an actual mage to tutor you," Master Tennival said. "Mostly in how to disguise your emotions, but in other ways as well if you'd like. I've been toying with the idea of asking to have someone sent to help Agrad—"

I shook my head and he stopped mid-sentence. "He won't trust that. You've seen how he is."

Master Tennival smiled patiently. "I know. You're probably right. Mostly, I was hoping for someone to guide me, so that I could point him to better books in my library, or recommend books I could borrow from elsewhere, so he'd have a rounded education. I'm not a teacher or tutor, but his appetite for knowledge is already insatiable on its own. Like you, I'm in over my head and need help."

His suggestion earlier that I should tell Lord Ceolwyn I couldn't do this because I was just a child had stung, had felt insulting and unnecessary, but this admission to feeling overwhelmed soothed that a bit. "You don't think I need help because I'm too young, then?"

"No. This has been hard on everyone, and none of us know what we're doing. Nobody's dealt with anything like this since the First Elemental War, and that wasn't exactly handled well. We can't afford that again, not with Verwyn, not when he's so fragile."

I looked Master Tennival over with a new appreciation. Maybe I shouldn't hold it against him that he'd been born just an ordinary human. I'd already started to forgive Agrad for it, and maybe I was being unfair. Maybe my parents were just...bad.

"Fine," I said. "If I get help, I'll stay. I'll keep the secrets that I have to keep, but I'm not going to lie to him anymore other than that. Agrad is a good person, and I like him."

"I like him, too," Master Tennival said. "He reminds me of how I used to be at his age, hundreds of years ago."

I laughed, thinking it was hyperbole. Grown-ups often made jokes like that.

But Master Tennival didn't laugh. He kept that same kind but weary smile on his face, and I didn't learn until later that it was the literal truth.

It was autumn, near Harvest, when I saw Visandra Cerine again. We saw each other in passing, she was with her father, and I wasn't sure how to react. I nodded as her eyes met mine and just watched from the other side of the road as a carriage trundled past. She waved me over as soon as the lane was clear with a bright smile and a tug on her father's sleeve to get him to stop.

I wasn't as enthusiastic as she was about meeting like this, but I walked over to them and offered up a bit of a smile. "Hello. I didn't expect to see you again."

Visandra grinned and grabbed both of my hands in hers faster than I could think to pull away. "It's so good to see you! I told you we might run into each other." She grinned from ear to ear, then looked at her father. "Papa, this is Ysili Ronar, the boy I helped last year. Ysili, this is my dad, Arment Cerine."

I took my hands back so that I could shake Master Cerine's enormous hand, then quickly shoved my fists in my pockets to keep them from being accosted again. "Pleased to meet you," I muttered at my feet.

"Ronar, nice," the man said in his deep and rumbly voice. "They're a good family, it's a good name. Vissy, I'll be in the shop if the two of you would like to reacquaint yourselves. Don't wander far."

I'm not sure if my shoes appreciated the scowl on my face, but I am fairly certain that Master Cerine and "Vissy" completely missed it. She pulled me over to a corner café and all but shoved me at one of the wrought iron torture devices they expected us to sit on. Maybe the shop owner thought it was a chair, but a tree stump in the woods was more comfortable than those things after five minutes.

"Your dad's wrong," I said, unsure if that whiny tone that spilled forth from my mouth was more petulant or sulky. Either description was probably apt.

She ignored me to order two hot ciders, smiling ever so politely at the waitress.

"It's not a good family, and it's not a good name," I continued, a bit more firmly and with an obvious undertone of anger. "You have no idea what—"

"Ysili, shut up a minute." Visandra smiled, head tilted to the side. "Every family is horrible in their own little ways, especially those of us descended from the first wizards. You're not alone in being miserable and used as a pawn."

"What?"

She kept her tone light and sweet, and somehow the smile

didn't falter. "I've had a very long trip with someone I'm not particularly fond of, and I'd like to not think of it for just a few minutes, so shut up if you can't say something pleasant. This is the first freedom I've had in months." Visandra then sat back in her chair, relaxed a bit, and stared at some point vaguely past the top of my head.

"Name of the gods, but you're bossy," I said with a roll of my eyes.

"It's called assertive, not bossy," she answered. "Bossy is for lower class girls, those of us in the upper class need to stand up for ourselves and be decisive." Visandra's smile brightened as the waitress returned, and she paid for the drinks with a chipper "Thank you". She slid one of the cups of cider closer to me, and the smile dropped. "You can't insult me, Ysili. You don't know how."

It seemed like such a strange thing to say. "I mean, I can. Apparently I just did, even though I was just stating a fact. You've been bossing me around. That makes you bossy."

She rolled her eyes.

"I didn't mean it to be mean," I said. "Well, maybe a little. You're being a little annoying, but I mean, it's nice to see you, and it's also kinda nice not to have to be in charge of everything and make all the decisions and be on my toes all the time. So, keep being bossy, I guess."

Visandra stared at me, hard, her expression intense for a minute. Then, she simply drank her cider and grinned.

"What are you smiling about?"

"Do you think that you're clever?" she asked.

I shrugged. "Not really. If I was clever I'd have kept my mouth shut and just enjoyed whatever coin you want to spend on me while pretending to like you. What I am is tired of pretending to be someone I'm not, and since I don't know if I'll ever see you again, you drew the short straw." I picked up the mug of cider, took a drink, and waited for her answer.

Her mouth tightened into a line that might technically qualify as a smile. "It seems we're both a bit cranky and tired, aren't we?"

"Did you want to talk about it?" I'm not sure why I asked, but I thought she wouldn't want to talk, and I'd look like I at least made an effort. Or, perhaps a few lessons in manners had stuck a little more solidly than I realized.

"My father's in negotiations for my eventual wedding. The day I turned thirteen he started pressuring me to write letters to about a dozen different men. Some of them are more than twice my age already. The only thing my family cares about is that they're also descended from a wizard or elemental."

"Oh."

"It's why he said what he did about your family."

I took another drink of my cider. She stared at me expectantly, so I sighed and set the cup aside. "It seems to mean a lot more to you and your family than it does for me. My parents abandoned me. I have no family, and my family name is just a way to distinguish me from any other Ysili."

"Right," she said with a wry twist to her lips. "You have no other distinguishing features. You clearly fade into any crowd."

That caught me by surprise from her. I didn't want to laugh, but it came upon me despite my wishes, in a sharp, short, burst.

Her eyes sparkled, and she seemed to soften around the edges as a genuine smile came over her. Then, her demeanor grew somber. "I'm sorry your family abandoned you, but you're better off without them. They've fallen out of favor because of what they did to you. I asked around about you after we met, and that incident was apparently a bit of hot gossip a few years ago."

"It doesn't matter, I don't care." The lie came easily to my lips. Not only because lies had become a way of life for me, but because how I felt about my family being a subject of gossip was none of her business. "So, tell me more about these arrangements your father has been trying to force you into."

Visandra's eyes darkened. I thought for a moment that she'd seen through my attempt to divert the conversation, but instead she launched into a tirade listing all the shortcomings of everyone she'd been forced to entertain.

Interlude Two

Are you writing about how we met?" Visandra leaned over Ysili's shoulder to take a look, but he covered up the page quickly. "That's so sweet."

"Don't look, it's not finished!" He set down his pen, warmth in his eyes as he took her hands in his, holding her away from the pages. "It's not a love note, I'm just trying to sort my thoughts, and remember everything we've been through to get here."

"So, more of Agrad than of me?" She tugged her hands as if to get free, but it instead pulled the two of them closer together. "It's not fair."

"He was my duty," Ysili said.

"He was your first love."

Ysili didn't deny it. Instead he pulled her onto his lap. "Be that as it may, I never would have found you without him. And there are things you give me that he never could have."

Visandra leaned in and gave him a quick kiss on the cheek. "You'd be more comfortable now if you'd stayed with him. You'd have a life of luxury as a wizard's favorite."

"I wouldn't have you." He let go of her hands so he could wrap his arms around her. "We're comfortable enough here, aren't we? If you want the luxury of being a wizard's lover, why don't you go and make a proposition to him yourself?"

"Oh no!" She giggled and wrapped her arms around his neck. "I couldn't stand being in a relationship with someone prettier than I am. I need all the attention for myself; you know how insecure I get."

"He was never prettier than you."

"Liar."

V – Two Hearts

Over time I grew comfortable in Cairnborough. I made many friends, learned many things. Half a year passed before I saw Visandra again, but we'd arranged to rendezvous ahead of time. Again our conversation was awkward and a bit frustrating, but at the end she said, "Hang in there. I know Agrad tries your patience, and this isn't how you want your life to go, but you're doing a great thing. Thank you."

They were exactly the words I needed to hear, and I never forgot them.

She was still such a small part of my life in those days, however. "Where have you been?" Agrad asked when I returned to our room. "Bad luck today?"

"Just got caught up in talking to a girl I know," I said as I took off my cloak.

"Not Tanyai this time?"

"No, thankfully. I think she's moved her attention to the baker's boy, Gren. He sneaks her day-old bread and pastries that don't sell. I think she finally got the idea that I'm just not interested in her." I grinned a bit. "You helped with that, of course."

"Did I?" He looked at me earnestly, eyelashes fluttering exactly the way an insecure young girl would if asking the same question. He was such a beautiful young lady in that moment that my breath caught in my throat. "Should I apologize for chasing her off? You could have played with her before cutting her loose, the way Bledig does with the girls who follow him around."

I scoffed. "I'm serious. I'm not interested in her, in anything to do with her. She was boring and never said a word but to agree with me or tell me how wonderful I was, even when I knew I wasn't."

"Isn't that what most boys want?"

"Is that what you would want? I'll bet if you told Tanyai your secret she'd follow you like a puppy."

He shook his head, his perfect black curls bouncing with the gesture. "I didn't like her, either. She was crude and ill-tempered behind your back. After seeing the truth of her, I

107

didn't want her even as a friend, but I put up with her for your sake."

"Don't put up with anyone for my sake." I sat down in my chair, a comfortable and cushy addition Agrad had brought in a few weeks before. It was a random gift that he used almost as often as I did. "I'm not worth the effort of dealing with backstabbing, vacuous humans and their devious ways."

Agrad bit his lower lip, worrying over it a while as he often did when he had a thought he wasn't sure he should share.

"Whatever it is, just say it."

He grimaced, but nodded. "Fine. Every once in a while, you say terrible things about humans."

"Right."

"But I'm human."

"I know," I said immediately, then realized what he meant. "Oh. You mean, why do I put up with you when I obviously despise humans?"

Agrad nodded, eyes wide. "Is it because I'm special?"

It's because I was being paid, I told myself. Because I was being paid, and because I had nothing better to do with my life at this point. I was setting myself up to lead a better life, eventually, by doing a favor to wizards and pretending to be one wizard's friend. That was all.

Wasn't it?

"I don't know if I'd call you special," I prevaricated. "There is something about you that's different, but you're right. You are human. I guess I don't mind it as much when it's you." I was somewhat surprised to find that that was true.

"Why?" He paused, then shook his head. "I mean, why do you hate humans so much? I don't want to be someone you hate for something I haven't done, you're my best friend."

I remembered the times he'd woken from nightmares and he'd crawled into bed with me for comfort, and all the times he hadn't woken from them and I sat next to him until the dreams had passed. I didn't do that for pay, or out of obligation. I did it because I knew what it felt like to suffer alone. Despite myself, I cared about him.

"I suppose I don't hate all humans," I said. It wasn't just Agrad I was thinking of. There was Visandra, too, and her kind words that were still fresh in my ears. "I'd have liked you more, sooner, if you'd just healed me back in the cave."

"But you'd have left, and I'd never have seen you again." He said it playfully, as if he was teasing.

But if he was teasing, why did it make me feel so sad for him?

"Magic healing or not, you helped me when I was in need. I wouldn't have just left. I'll stay by your side until you're sick of me."

In that moment, I meant it.

Agrad tilted his head to the side, then smiled. "Thanks. Sorry I didn't heal you. I'm still no good at it, but maybe I should have tried harder. I was just scared."

"Well, there's nothing to be scared of, now." My duplicity caught up to me as I said it. It wasn't a lie, no one was going to touch him here, but it was because the worst of his fears had already come true, and he just didn't know it. "I'm taking a shift in the kitchen tonight. I'll see you later." I picked myself up and patted him on the head as if he were a puppy.

"I already paid extra so you don't have to," he blurted out as I closed the door.

I walked away. I needed something to do with my hands.

109

Something to do so that I wouldn't have to let my thoughts circle around how I didn't deserve a friend as blindly trusting as he was.

What I couldn't get out of my head was this idea that I'd maybe wasted my energy by hating humans without cause, simply because a few had done terrible things to me. It felt childish, never mind that I'd been a small child when the idea had first taken hold. A few days passed, and I started to feel embarrassed. I'd done what my parents had done in discounting others by how they were born rather than who they were.

"You look unusually contemplative today."

Paelloret had come up and sat next to me in the common room, catching me by surprise. I'd been so lost in thought I hadn't even noticed him.

"If you say so." I'd have to watch that, out here. I had money, and we lived with some of the most talented pickpockets in the city. I couldn't be paranoid all the time, but relaxing too much in the common room was probably not the smartest thing I could have done. "I suppose I have a lot on my mind."

"Girl problems?" He grinned. "Will Agrad be available soon?"

I rolled my eyes. "If you like her that much, go ahead and try. I won't get in her way." I waved a hand toward our room, even though Agrad was with Master Tennival at the time. As he was almost always. "If you can catch her attention, that is.

She's always working." I rolled my eyes. "But, no, there's no problems. We're fine aside from never seeing each other."

"Hmmm." He looked over at our door thoughtfully, then back at me. "If it's not her, or the other girl you were seen with, what is it?"

"What, Visandra?" Damn it, would I have to meet her clandestinely? That was ridiculous. "She's my cousin, sort of, but not really. And she's just a human—" but I stopped myself as the words came out, because that was the problem.

"So is Agrad." Paelloret leaned in closer, a twinkle in his eyes. "Trust me, if I didn't know she'd be a grandmother by the time I'm ready to settle down, her being human would be easy for me to overlook."

"It hasn't been easy for me." I slumped in my seat and kept my voice low. "I'm working on it, I get so angry about humans, about how they've treated me, and it all comes out at Agrad, and even at Visandra sometimes."

He didn't say anything at first. Then, he nodded and put a hand on my shoulder. "You're not alone there, a lot of us with other parentages are getting a bit unhappy with certain human behaviors. But… aren't you mostly human?"

"Well," I started, with a hesitant nod, "I think my mother was completely human, but I don't remember much about her."

"Are your parents dead, too?"

"No." I almost left it there, almost stopped talking. I actually almost stood and left to be completely honest. In the end I was just so tired of lies and secrets that I decided to let out the raw and honest truth. "They didn't want me, once they had a real child."

Paelloret nodded. "Humans killed my parents, ten years

ago. However, Mistress Relata saved me, kept the men from killing me as well, and brought me here so I'd be safe since I was too young to go home alone. I'll probably leave, try to return home to Shalysalaianleth, in another ten years. That will be...five years after you and Agrad leave, I think? But I've started to wonder, where are my aunts or uncles? Where are my grandparents? I've seen human children rescued from this place by extended family, but I am still here."

"Elves are bad, too?"

"Anyone can be bad, and anyone can be good." He shrugged. "You can hate everyone who reminds you of those who have wronged you, if you want. That's your decision. However, the people who deserve your ire won't care if you hate them, and those who don't deserve it are the only ones who will be hurt."

"Your family is stupid for not coming to find you," I said. It was the only thing I could think to say. "You're smart, and you're wise, and I'm sorry your parents are dead."

"I agree," Paelloret said with a lopsided grin. "I'm sorry my parents are dead, too. But, as for the rest of my family, they're probably blissfully unaware my parents are even gone. It's been less than a century, after all." He rolled his eyes then. "It's so odd, being raised like this. The children who were here when I arrived have children of their own now. My old friends have no time for me, and I'm still growing up. It's like you're all cats, but smarter. You're grown adults in the blink of an eye."

"And we're all going to die in the blink of an eye, too," I said. "Does that make you lonely?"

He nodded. "I try not to think about it, but it's probably why my parents didn't have many human friends. Not many elves are raised by humans, just like very few humans have been raised by elves, and this is probably why. I've had to mature beyond my age, trying to keep up and trying to survive. I suppose I could safely go to my homelands now; I know where to go and how to get there, and I'm clever enough to make it. But what then? I'll be treated as lesser than. I'll be coddled and my opinions will be dismissed. Here I'm an authority and a fixture. All the other kids turn to me for help and advice. At home I'd be a pathetic baby."

Yeah, that made sense. I'd already had to deal with that kind of thing by my tutor, by Master Tennival, and by hundreds of perfect strangers I'd met in the city. If I'd spent ten years being forced to learn at the speed of a human, but aging like an elf, and knowing I had another decade of being treated like an infant, I'd probably be reluctant to go home, too.

Paelloret smiled and elbowed me in the side. "Feeling better?"

"A bit."

"Good. Can I borrow a few nubs? Or a wheel if you've got it?"

I rolled my eyes and fished three nubs out of my pocket. "You earned it. Thanks."

"Nice. If you're giving out coin, I'll sit and listen more often."

It was the beginning of madness, of a sort. What Paelloret had said made sense, and it wouldn't be fair to treat people who had done nothing wrong as if they were the people who had hurt me. From the moment I set that aside, I let myself see Agrad differently.

We got older, and Agrad only grew prettier, which was problem number one. Problem two was Agrad was fairly witty and amusing, compassionate to a fault, and generally oblivious. He was fun to be around, nice to look at, and as far as I could tell was not even the least bit interested in moving things between us beyond friendship.

The third problem was the worst. Agrad was clever, more so than me, and it always irritated me after we'd have a serious discussion where I'd walk away and realize hours, or sometimes days, later that he hadn't answered the question I'd asked, and I hadn't even realized it.

He offered me small consolations at times. We'd started an argument about how I never saw him anymore. Somewhere in the middle, while I was trying to get Agrad to open up and talk to me about all the things I already knew so maybe I wouldn't have to lie to him anymore, and he pulled off his dress. Everything flew from my mind in that moment and all I could do was stare, wishing this was a prelude to something more intimate, while I was slapped in the face with how thin and boyish he looked without layers of clothes to make him into just another young lady in the town. I wanted to hold him and tell him everything and comfort him and tell him it would all be okay, swear I would protect him for the rest of his life, and instead I all but ran from the room.

As consolation for this fight, he offered to introduce me to Master Tennival, giving me only one small thing I no longer had to hide.

That was the thing. I couldn't touch him as long as all I

had to offer him was a series of lies.

Visandra, on the other hand, knew everything. I never had to hide who I was or what I was feeling. We didn't always get along, she wasn't always nice, and sometimes my jokes fell flat. She was voluptuous where Agrad was willowy. Visandra was fierce and determined, where Agrad was withdrawn and would go along with just about anything but still somehow get his way in the end. They were night and day, and as I let myself get to know them better without resenting their humanity, I found myself drawn to both of them for completely different reasons.

Years went by.

This didn't resolve.

I exchanged letters with Visandra. She told me about all the suitors she rebuffed, and teasingly asked if I was jealous. I told her about Agrad's latest jokes, Bledig's increasing clout in dangerous circles, and Paelloret's oddly incongruous wisdom mixed with sudden bouts of silly chaos. At some point I told her of my unrequited feelings for Agrad, and she told me that one suitor she'd been set up with was secretly a woman, and how confused she was that the prospect intrigued her. It opened an exchange of ideas that left us both a little more open about what prospects we might entertain in the future.

With every letter I felt closer to her. She was my true best friend.

Still, despite the lies, I thought that I'd win Agrad's affection in the end.

I thought that Visandra would get married to some proper mage or diplomat.

Apparently, I had no gift for prophesy.

VI – Memory Day

Everyone I've talked to remembers where they were, what they were doing on Memory Day 333. The sensation of hopelessness, helplessness, and despair that overcame everyone that day was unforgettable. For most, that's all they know about that day. Just a universal malaise that passed as abruptly as it came. A great mystery of our times.

For me, the morning started much like any other. "It's Memory Day," Agrad said, wrapping a thick shawl around his shoulders as he stepped toward the door. "Wish me luck."

"I can walk with you," I said, though I was adding a bit more to my latest letter to Visandra. "I know how you hate facing those paintings." Every year, just before Memory Day, Master Tennival would put up paintings of the wizards, and every year Agrad would come home looking haunted and morose. The nightmares intensified this time of year, and I wondered if seeing Lord Ceolwyn's face still stirred terror in him.

"Don't worry," he said. "I think I can handle it this year. It's paint and canvas. It's not like the wizards themselves will step through and apprehend me." He laughed lightly, sounding like a caged bird. "Besides, most of them are long dead and reborn by now. I feel almost like I'm getting away with something, hiding in the employ of their favorite artist."

"I'm almost finished with this letter," I said. "If you want to wait a moment, it would be no bother."

"It's fine," he said gently. Agrad walked over and put a

hand on my shoulder. "Stay here until I return? I'll probably be early today, since Master Tennival doesn't usually paint on Memory Day. We'll go to Cairnfeld and talk a bit, then I'll be back."

I nodded and smiled up at him. His black hair was tied up just so, perfectly coifed and framing his face like a sparkling night sky embracing the moon. He looked at peace, and I believed that this day would be one like any other. "I'll see you later."

Agrad left and I returned to my letter, shoulder still warm where his hand had been.

I've reached the age of majority, and Agrad will soon. Perhaps I should just be bluntly honest about my feelings for him, then tell him the truth. All of the truth. Forget what the others want, or expect, of me. I don't want to live like this anymore. Will you console me when he turns me away and laughs in my face? If I survive the truth-telling portion of my confession, of course. He might erase me from the world entirely, in which case I suppose I'll have no need of consolation.

There it was in ink, and I couldn't take it back without re-writing a great deal of the rest of the letter. If I scribbled it out Visandra would hound me in person to tell her what it had said. She understood, though, and put up with my dramatics with a smile and a roll of the eyes.

Don't start mourning yet, of course. If I haven't found the courage to tell him in all these years, I'm sure it won't happen until long after your next visit. Gods and wizards willing this letter will reach you a week or two before you leave for the summer estate, and

117

you can laugh at me and my antics in person.
Your Faithful Friend,
Ysili Ronar

I ended it there and sealed the envelope, thus proving I was doubly a coward for not telling Visandra how I felt about her. Then again, I had my whole life ahead of me to make one or the other of them miserable with my company. Or so I thought.

Of course, I'd left all of that unwritten until after Agrad had left. He knew there was a girl I'd been writing to, but he didn't know who, and it hadn't seemed to matter to him at all. I'd been so casual about it that I'm not sure he'd cared. It was probably for the best, because any hint of curiosity or jealousy would have opened the floodgates and I'd have told him everything then and there.

If Lord Ceolwyn had shot me when I'd done nothing wrong, what would he do if I'd outright disobeyed him? If I destroyed his plans by revealing the truth, and ran away with his prize? How much more would I suffer once we were caught?

It was a sobering thought. It was the real reason I hadn't confessed my emotions, my motivations, or anything real about me. What absolute disaster awaited me if I said the wrong thing? That was, of course, if Agrad maintained enough control of his own magic upon hearing the truth from me.

If.

I'd had a growing doubt that Agrad could, actually, do anything as cataclysmic as destroy his hometown as Lord Ceolwyn had said. What if it had been something else? Some coincidental magical discharge? I couldn't imagine Agrad doing something so destructive. He was sweet and kind. He had a silly, ridiculous sort of humor, quirky and sweet. He was easily embarrassed and blushed innocently at tiny things I'd long since become completely used to.

The Agrad I knew wasn't dangerous. Shy, perhaps, but not dangerous.

But maybe I didn't know him at all. He lied to me as often as I lied to him. The difference, or so I thought, was that I knew how often he lied.

Didn't I?

I tidied the room while my thoughts circled through these well-worn paths. It wasn't something I usually thought to do, but I wanted Agrad to be put at ease as much as I could. He'd put on a brave face before he left, but I could tell that deep down seeing those paintings still bothered him, and I'd be comforting him through nightmares again. The less day to day mundane stuff he felt the need to worry over, the better.

Somewhere in that time I stopped. I sat down and nursed the realization that I'd never have an actual future with Agrad. It was a thought that crept up slowly at first, but it became a weight that pushed me down into the chair, harder and harder, until I could barely breathe. What I wanted was hopeless. I wasn't worthy of Agrad. I wasn't even worthy of Visandra. I was a creature, a creation, not a person, and nothing I did mattered.

Agrad had a future as a wizard, he was an elemental, and he was about to be of age to take his country and learn to rule. Soon, he wouldn't have time for me. He'd realize I wasn't worth the effort. He'd find out the truth about me and he'd never want to see me again. What was the point in cleaning the room, when just by being his friend I was betraying him?

On top of that, I was also reaching beyond my station by so much as speaking to Visandra. She was a direct descendant of one of the original wizards. I may have had the last name of one of those wizards, but I had no idea if I had the same blood in my veins. My father had disavowed me, had said I was not family, and I'd been abandoned so young that I had no idea if my mother was also of such celebrated heritage or if she'd been picked at random off the street. Either way, I'd been cast aside. I was not their family. I was a diversion until they could have the real thing.

Somewhere out there, I had a sister. She would bear the family name. She would have the prestige that has been denied me. Did she even know I existed? Would she care?

Would she think of me as my parents had thought of me? A thing that was once discarded.

In this doubt and insignificance, Agrad returned. I couldn't even muster the energy to look up at him, I felt so despondent.

Maybe, if I didn't move, he wouldn't notice what a horrid monstrosity I was.

I sat, barely blinking, as he moved through the room and gathered the meager items he valued. Everything went into a pack that he slung over one shoulder, and then he left me some money he'd saved.

Like I was some whore he was paying because he was done with me.

He walked over to me, kissed me on the cheek, and stared at me with misery that echoed my own. "I'm so sorry," he whispered. "I think I fell in love with you, but you deserve someone better. A real lady. Someone who can give you a family, a home, and stability. I'm not who you think I am. I'm a terrible thing, and I'll never deserve someone like you. If you're lucky, you'll never have to see me again."

I remember the words as if they are etched into my soul. His despair was my despair, and the hopelessness was such that I couldn't muster the will to meet his eyes. If I'd had the power, I may have jumped from a great height just to bring an end to the pain my heart bore, to bring an end to my life and the suffering it caused.

Even after Agrad left I found myself locked in that stupor, unable to call out after him or follow him to stop him from running away.

The feeling released me from its grip in a sudden instant and I bolted to my feet. I didn't stop to think, I just ran. Everyone I ran past looked like they were waking up from a deep sleep, from the great room in the boarding house to the streets. It was eerie.

I didn't have time to think about it. I had to find Agrad.

There was no time to question where I was running to. I just knew. I was at the wall that surrounded the gravesite that was Cairnfeld before I realized why I knew where to find him.

Around me, the air was so full of magic that I stopped in my tracks.

It wasn't just Agrad.

Krecek Ceolwyn was there along with others, all of them standing around the large cairn stones in the center of the vast field. All of them wielded the same amount of power, and I felt the full scope of the insignificance of the small amount of magic I could cast.

It wasn't a hopeless feeling, like what had overwhelmed me before. I was aware of my talent and my worth, but I was also aware that these people gathered before me were gods barely contained by mortal flesh. They were performing a ritual, and Agrad lay still at their feet, bloody and bruised, dress torn and covered in mud and grass.

He wasn't dead. His chest rose and fell, and his unique flavor of magic was woven into whatever ritual they performed.

All I could do was stare. I was unwilling to approach for fear of interrupting and being swatted absently like a fly at a feast. However, my entire purpose for almost a decade had been to watch over Agrad, so I felt constrained to stay, to await orders on what to do next.

I was a marionette, hung beside the stage by a nail between acts. With no one to pull my strings I had no initiative, no thought of how to behave on my own.

Then Krecek walked over, and without a word I followed him.

I hadn't known he still owned the strings.

A servant was sent to gather my belongings. I didn't say goodbye to my friends.

I'd already heard that everyone had felt the same crushing despair and feeling of insignificance by the time Krecek sat with me to eat. I was completely mentally off balance, reeling from the events.

"Will Agrad be okay?" I asked after a long silence.

"It takes more than that to kill a wizard." Krecek's smile was tight-lipped and disappeared in an instant. He only glanced at me for the duration of it, before turning his gaze on the plate before him again. "Physically, he should recover by morning. Mentally, well, I suppose time will tell." He toyed with a spear of roasted asparagus on the plate for a few minutes, then set his fork aside. "Naran said that Agrad seemed to have adjusted well while living here. That he'd made friends."

"I made friends," I said. "We included him, but he never went out of his way to meet anyone on his own."

"Hm." Krecek sat back, eyebrows furrowed. "Still, he was well adjusted, wasn't he?"

I thought of the nightmares. The mercurial mood swings if I pressed him too much to talk about the past. The time Agrad spent withdrawn into a book, avoiding everyone.

"As well adjusted as anyone I've known."

It was true, if it wasn't entirely honest. Everyone had their dark moments, their secrets, their tempers. I wasn't going to lie, but I didn't want Krecek thinking Agrad was some dangerous monster who needed to be locked away, either.

"That's not the endorsement you think it is," Krecek said as he refilled his wine glass. He'd somehow caught my prevarication. "Never mind, I'm sure Byrek can handle him. He's handled every other Verwyn, even at their worst."

I nodded, despite not knowing who or what he was talking about. I didn't entirely feel like he was talking to me, but using me to have his own conversation. So, I sat back and waited. The food before me hadn't interested me, though the quality was better than I'd had since I'd lived in Anogrin. I was so emotionally numb that flavor didn't reach me.

It took a while, but Krecek relaxed and sighed heavily before he began speaking again. "This isn't the end I'd hoped

123

for, but it's also not what I'd been afraid it could become. At least it's over. Agrad is safe, and he can learn how to rule if by some chance he wants to. Or is able to."

Over.

It was all over.

"You should get some sleep. We have a long journey ahead of us."

What else could I do? Wait here for Agrad to wake up and then follow him like a lost puppy? He'd already walked out on me once that day. I didn't want to give him a chance to reject me again. I rubbed at my calf; at the spot I'd been hit by the arrow. There was still a small scar on both sides of my leg.

Somehow, it still hurt less than the words Agrad had said before he walked out the door.

VII – The Guard

The road to Anogrin wasn't long, taking a handful of days to reach by carriage. Still, it was enough time that the stunned numbness receded. None of us spoke much, so I lived in my own head, recalling certain moments of that day over and over again, without interruption.

If I had gone with Agrad, how would things be different? Could I have stopped him? Could I have offered him the comfort and strength he needed to not lose control?

Or was it a gift that I hadn't been there? If I'd been there, would he have found out the truth? If he had found out the truth I might have saved the world from a shared mental malaise, but he would have killed me for certain.

Would that have been a bad thing?

I glanced at Krecek at times as we rode, and my mind stirred up other memories. I'd been in so much awe, I'd had so much respect, when I was little. When he'd been the only parent I had left. In my thoughts he'd always been Lord Ceolwyn, the great and kind wizard who had given me a reason to live. Now he was Krecek inside the confines of my own skull, and the name was accompanied with a mix of terror and contempt. He'd been taller than me the last time I'd seen him. Now my nose and a bit more cleared the top of his head. Could I rest my chin upon it if I tried? Would he destroy me if I tried?

The winding road up the mountain took the most time, and I was relieved at first when we reached the city gates. By the time we'd hit the inner wall of the castle my heart was pounding and I could hardly breathe. We came to a stop in the courtyard and I was the last out the carriage door, clinging to the frame for many heartbeats before I forced my feet to move.

And then I faltered.

What was I doing here? I'd set myself up with a false choice between Krecek and Agrad. I'd chosen the one who had hurt me longer ago, true, but they'd both betrayed me. I didn't need to be here.

"No." The word just slipped out.

Krecek stopped and turned to look at me with his head cocked to the side. He waited, staring for a few moments, then came to my side when I didn't move. "No? What's wrong?"

"I don't want to be here." It wasn't exactly true. The palace wasn't the problem. So I tried to put it into words, and the words came out as accusations. "What do you want from me? Why did you bring me here? Did you manipulate my feelings, make me numb until we got here, the way *he* did?"

"Ysili." His brow furrowed, and he looked up at me with concern. "No. I would never do that to you. I only wanted to bring you home. Why are you suddenly afraid of —" He cut himself off, realization written on his face. "Me. Oh."

"You hurt me. Of course I'm afraid of you after that! I was doing you a favor, and you shot me. Would you want to live in someone's home if they'd done that to you?"

"I did what I had to." Again, though, he stopped himself and shook his head. "I'm sorry, I should have come up with a different plan. I was terrified Agrad would run again, or worse. Worse, like what he just did a few days ago."

I scowled. "Do you want to see the scar you left me as a reminder all these years? The arrow went straight through, right to the fletching before it stopped. It still hurts sometimes, because Agrad was too terrified to use any magic and I couldn't do much for myself." Now that I could feel my emotions again the floodgates were opened and I couldn't stop the torrent.

"You're right," he said. "How do I make this up to you?"

"You shot me with an arrow." I didn't want an apology. I was trembling with how overwhelmed I was, ready to walk away, to live off the land, to beg for a living or become a thief in reality if this is how things had to play out.

"I had to make it believable, that you were on the run also, or he might have killed you."

"He might have killed me anyway, and you still SHOT me with an ARROW!"

"Is there anything I can do? Money? Titles? Women

falling at their knees to please you? What do you want from me? Name it!"

"I want you to let me shoot you with an arrow." Revenge. I wanted revenge.

"What?"

"Let me shoot you. I won't even demand you sit and rot in a cave for days while some other wizard refuses to heal you. Just let me shoot you with an arrow."

"What good would that do? A simple arrow can't kill me."

"I don't want to kill you! I didn't die. I don't want you to die. But I damn well am not going to forgive you unless I know, with my own eyes, that you know what you put me through!"

Krecek stared at me, his face grim, but after a time he nodded. "I owe you that much." He called over a young squire. "Bring me a bow and a quiver of arrows." The boy ran off at full speed, and Krecek met my eyes. "No tricks of magic. A real arrow that I'd use for any hunting trip. And I'll let you be the only one to heal me, as you see fit."

We waited in silence, staring at each other, until the boy returned with the items. With a gesture from Krecek the boy handed them to me, wide-eyed. I examined the bow, took an arrow and examined it, tested the sharpness and solidity of the arrow tip with my finger, and finally nodded in satisfaction. It was real enough.

I nocked the bow and took a few steps backward, taking aim at his leg. I didn't really know what I was doing, hadn't had a chance to hold a bow and arrow since I was small, since I'd lived here, and I'd never been very good at it. I don't think I looked too awkward with it. The string was harder to pull than I remembered, and it wasn't a child's practice weapon. It felt strange to hold the arrow in place while pulling back, but at least I didn't make a fool of myself by letting it swing wildly in my fingers.

Then, I slowly relaxed my grip without letting the arrow fly. Krecek had grimaced, but he hadn't flinched. He'd waited for me to do to him what he'd done to me. For that reason, I didn't even attempt to fix my posture and follow through.

"Never mind," I said and shoved the whole thing at the boy who had delivered the bow and arrows. "It was a stupid idea anyway. Hurting you won't fix what you did."

"Will you stay and accept my protection, at least?"

I thought it over a while before I finally nodded. "Sure."

It was frustration at my own ineptitude with the bow as much as anything that drew me to the courtyard every morning where the current guards practiced, and the aspiring guards trained. Krecek had been good enough to shoot me while I was fleeing, and he was a great wizard. If he could wield both weapons and magic, I had no excuse. I was still trying to decide if I should stay or slip away in the middle of the night, but either way I thought I should learn as many survival skills as I could manage. I didn't want to fall into my own helplessness ever again.

I could have been a mage. I could have been a spellsmith. But there was peace to be found in forcing my body to act, to react, and learn the motions that grew into skills. In some countries a "mere guard" was looked down upon for choosing brawn over brain, but in Ceolwyn we were taught the

128

strength that combining the two could bring. Even soldiers who couldn't do magic were still given tools to use that combined magic items with their physical prowess.

Before I knew it, months had passed while I wavered. While I learned.

I was as surprised as anyone when Reyen, the old commander, sat down with me. He asked if I wanted to learn to fight, or if I wanted to join the guard.

"I just want something to do," I said. "Something tangible that won't have me cooped up indoors or on my ass all the time. I keep being pushed to be a mage, and I don't mind using a bit of magic now and then, but it's not who I want to be."

"Still trying to find who you are, hm?"

I nodded.

"You're good enough, you learn quick enough, that we'd take you if you want," he said.

It was a nice complement, and I smiled. "Thanks. Isn't it a boring job, though?"

He looked taken aback. "What?"

"Well, any guard that works for a wizard must feel useless. It's an honorary sort of job, isn't it? It's not like they can be hurt by any normal person. They can do anything."

"You think we only guard Lord Ceolwyn?"

"You don't?"

He shook his head. "No. Not even remotely." He looked off across the room, eyes narrowed in thought. "The story is, back when the wizards first took power, Lord Ceolwyn took in a young girl who had run away from home to work for him. It was before the palace had been built, before the guard had been established. An assassin had been sent by priests, and he had given the girl his own bed. She was stabbed through the heart while he slept, and he only barely managed to save her life while the assassin got away." He shrugged. "That's how we started, or what I was told. We pledge ourselves to each other, not to him. We're here in service to the mortals under his roof, and to protect the halls we live within."

That caught me by surprise. "There are always guards around Krecek, though."

"When you see him, of course." His eyes twinkled in amusement. "We've been there to protect you from his enemies. You and anyone else at his side. He can take care of himself, believe me. Lord Ceolwyn has saved my life as often as I've saved the lives of his companions." Commander Rayen then stood and brushed his hands off on his pants. "If you want to protect others from what it means to be too close to those in power, we'd welcome you. If that's not what you want out of your life, if you have other goals, you're welcome to go elsewhere. Give it some thought. I'll see you later."

He left me with my thoughts.

A week later, I started training in earnest.

Interlude Three

Visandra kissed Ysili on the ear, startling him out of his concentration, disrupting his flow. "Remember how you told me not to read this yet, because you're not finished?"

Ysili frowned. "You looked, didn't you?"

Her laughter was immediate, and took the sting out of the idea of her reading his most private thoughts. "I've been standing behind you for a while now. You said to give you a moment, then forgot I was here. What else was I going to do?"

"You could have walked away and come back later."

"I was waiting until it looked like you finished your thought. Which was now."

He leaned against her and then twisted to wrap an arm around her hips. "Well, what do you think?"

"I think you should skip all the training. It's boring to anyone who hasn't been through it, and anyone who has will already know what it was like." She grinned and kissed the top of his head. "You're about to get to the good part. Just skip to that."

Ysili nodded. "I don't think I would have written all of that down. I've skipped a lot of details, trying to sort my emotions out. Exercising and learning how not to stab myself with a sword is something I did, not something I thought about." He held her closer and breathed in the scent of her, clung to the soft warmth of her. "I still think it was the best decision I made, and I don't have any conflicting feelings over it. If I hadn't joined the guard, we never would have been married."

"To think I almost chose Drav Anates over you. Can you imagine?"

"All too well," he said, pulling back with a frown. "He was a good man, and I know he'd have treated you well, but I'm selfish. I need you more than he did."

"And I needed you more than I needed him," she said gently. Visandra then sat in his lap and kissed his cheek. "I'm glad everything worked out this way."

VIII – Visandra

It took me a while to think to send a letter to Visandra and to remember that I hadn't sent her the letter I'd finished on Memory Day. I sent her that one as well as a note to tell her where I was and a promise to explain later.

An explanation that took quite a while, because I was going to bed as exhausted as I could manage. I wasn't particularly eager to talk about any of it, let alone think about it.

I didn't hear from her for a while after I sent my letter, and in passing I wondered what could cause the delay. Was she angry with me for how long it had taken me to send my last reply, or had something gone wrong? I had to put it from my mind, though. I had too many sudden responsibilities to spend my scant free time worrying.

One thing was a constant in palace life. Visitors. There seemed to be demands on Lord Ceolwyn's time constantly, with people in and out, from what seemed like all corners of the world.

There were the local politicians, of course, visiting regularly and sending their messengers out regularly. The diplomats from other countries flying the flags of their homeland and arriving by coaches that nearly rivaled a wizard's own. They stayed sometimes for years, and their messengers were in and out at all hours, delivering only missives for their lords with a staunch refusal to carry anything extra for any amount of coin. They all seemed to be descendants of some wizard or elemental at some point, like my parents had been. Then once a season, Lord Ceolwyn would welcome commoners in with their gold favors, accepting their coins in exchange for a boon.

I watched out for the common messengers the most, hoping for word from either Agrad or Visandra. I'd sent them each awkward letters explaining where I was and that I was safe.

Agrad never sent me a single word in reply.

Then, eventually, correspondence from Visandra came. I rushed to my room to read it in private.

I needn't have bothered. It was an engagement announcement.

Not exactly something that called for privacy.

But I took advantage of the solitude to stare into the nothingness for a while.

Just months ago I had two friends and my freedom.

In that moment, I realized that I had nothing at all.

Visandra,

I shouldn't be shocked to receive your invitation. Your father has been hard at work to find you a worthy suitor for so many years, so it's natural you've found someone worthy of your attentions at last. Congratulations.

My life is still very busy, very hectic, but I would be a poor friend indeed if I didn't reply as quickly as possible to your news. I promise a genuine and proper correspondence as soon as I am able to string more than a handful of words together at a time.

Let me know if you have plans to come to Anogrin. I'd love to see a friendly face again. I think being so high up in the mountains has turned every disposition chilly, and the summer here is too short to thaw anyone's tempers. I don't know if you'll have time to travel, but the warmth of a smile would be most welcome.
Your Friend,
Ysili Ronar

The reply came shockingly fast.

Dearest Ysili,
I'll be in Anogrin perhaps within days of you receiving this letter. Patience, my friend. I will explain all in person.
Yours ever,
Vissy

It was a completely garbage reply, if you asked me at the time. From calling me "dearest" to signing it off like she did, I wanted to climb the walls in frustration. A wedding invitation should be a plain enough rejection on its own, and she should just leave me to heal my emotional wounds alone, shouldn't she? What else was there to explain? I know I didn't have any claim on her. I didn't deserve her. Still, it ached just the same.

Krecek was away, or busy, or something. I'm not sure, I just remember that I couldn't go to him for advice or help. Hell, maybe I was just feeling blindly resentful still and didn't want to speak to him. What I remember most of waiting for Visandra after receiving that letter was an overwhelming feeling of loneliness. Maybe I could have written another letter to Agrad, but I didn't want to. He'd made his decision to leave me behind, and a not insignificant part of me was still

134

flatly terrified of what I'd seen him do. The emotions had felt like my own self-loathing and insignificance, so how would I even know if he decided to turn me into a puppet?

Wizards were quietly terrifying, I thought to myself, even when they acted pleasant. Were there no limits to what they could do, even untrained? I was glad he was locked away, relieved at the thought I might never see him again. I missed him, but at times I questioned even that, because what if that wasn't my emotion at all, but something he'd unknowingly planted in my head.

The longer I wallowed in those thoughts, the more I hated him. I didn't have anyone to temper it, to help me be rational about it, and the feeling grew.

The more I missed him, the more I resented him.

Wrapped in my fears and loneliness, it didn't matter that Visandra would be here within days. I trained with the soldiers, I ate, and when I had nothing left to do I wallowed in my emotions until sleep took hold and started the cycle again.

Somehow, I was caught by surprise when Visandra did arrive. I was in the courtyard, a sweaty and dusty mess after working out, when I spotted her on horseback next to an older man as finely dressed as she was. She allowed him to help her down with what seemed forced warmth, though it could have been the odd restraint expected of those who saw themselves as the upper class.

Her hand did not linger within his, and she hurriedly shook dust from her skirts and shook her head. This was followed by an exchange of words I couldn't hear, and a paige rushed forward to gather their names and pass along knowledge of their presence within the walls of the palace. A carriage trundled up behind them after a time, which prompted Visandra to turn to look and then smile.

And then she saw me.

Her smile vanished.

She nodded to me, lifted a hand, then turned to her companion to point me out. His jaw clenched, and he pulled her toward him possessively.

Was this the, to use the word loosely, *man* she was engaged to? I had an instant dislike for him, and I felt a smirk forming as an idea struck me. I dashed over to them, waving and calling her name across the distance.

"Vissy! Over here! I've missed you so, it's been months. So glad you got my last letter."

She arched an eyebrow, and her lips formed half a smirk momentarily, but that was her only reaction.

"Oh, don't hug me, I'm a sweaty mess." I lifted my arm and pretended to sniff, then wrinkled my nose. "Honestly, your timing is terrible. So, let me guess, this is...oh, how embarrassing, I've forgotten your name. I've only seen it on the wedding announcement after all."

"Drav Anates." He extended a hand to shake, and I made a show of wiping my hands on my dusty pants to wipe away sweat. This prompted hesitation and disgust, but he had made the gesture first, and apparently he was determined to see it through.

Well, even after wiping off my hands, they were sweaty and warm. It made his hand seem limp and slippery as a fish, possibly an impression that was contributed by his distaste.

"I'm Ysili."

"Yes, Visandra has told me all about you. At length."

Drav sounded mildly irritated at this, but I was shocked into forgetting my posturing for a moment.

136

"Vis?" I frowned. "Are you trying to make your fiancé jealous?"

"The opposite," she insisted. "The last time we spoke you were still hopeless over Agrad."

Drav started to say something, but then snapped his mouth shut as someone approached.

"Lord Anates, Lady Cerine, I am to show you to your suite."

I vaguely recognized the young lady who had approached. She was one of the many maids who usually did their best to seem invisible around the rest of us. Or perhaps they all were simply hiding from me and my oddness.

"I'll take my leave of the two of you then," I said hastily as I took two steps backward away from them.

"I'll find you later, Ysili," Visandra said. Was it a threat? A promise?

I lifted a hand and turned away. She would make due on those words, and I wanted to show her the best of what she'd be losing.

I'd expected her to pound on my door as I was changing, or something equally embarrassing. Instead, she sat beside me at supper, with Drav on the other side of her. It wasn't horribly formal, but I was still shocked that they weren't seated closer to the head of the table. The dining hall was nearly always full and bustling with activity and conversation. I tended to keep to myself, watching how everyone else behaved, observing who was socializing and who was being snubbed, keeping a mental tally of who was coming ahead or falling behind in their social games. I hadn't expected to find myself among the players.

"Lady Cerine, Lord Anates, what a surprise to see you at the humble end of the room." I grinned, showing no obeisance other than using the titles that had been applied to them before, and that was said with a humor that robbed it of respect. "So, are you an ambassador, Drav?"

"I told you we should be at the—" Drav started, but Visandra cut him off.

"Lord Ceolwyn isn't here, and I want to sit with my friend. I told you, I don't care what our proper place may or may not be."

I liked that. She chose to sit here, with me, among those who weren't status seekers. I'd also made a decision to sit where I wanted in this room full of chaos, in a spot where I could observe rather than be observed. Did she understand that, though? Visandra was sharp witted enough that she might, and she sometimes understood what drove me more than I did.

"Yes," Drav finally said, a bit curt. "I am an ambassador. I am in service to Lord Lorwyn, serving in Eudwyn. It's customary to tour the other countries before a big event."

Lorwyn. I looked at Visandra curiously. "You're from Lorwyn, aren't you? Is that how the two of you met? Is he also descended from one of the original wizards?"

"I'm not," Drav answered for himself. "I just have a status great enough to satisfy her father's stringent standards."

Visandra nodded. "My father arranged it all, and this time I wasn't given much choice."

"Any choice," Drav leaned in as he spoke, keeping his

volume low. "He's embarrassed that a girl of her age and status has not yet wed, and has offered an uncomfortably large dowery. I'd expected a domineering shrew of an older woman, before we met."

I choked. "What?"

"It's ridiculous." Visandra's tone was a mix of subdued mortification and indignation. "You've met him. You saw how desperate he was when I was barely nubile. Everything is about status and appearances to him. There's no one to hold him back and calm him down, so he just grasps an idea until the world submits. It's the lack of magic that has him in a panic, as if that is enough to make me a lesser being."

I rolled my eyes. "He's probably pushing your potential suitors away more than you are."

"Indeed," Drav raised his glass to the idea and took a deep drink. "That's the impression I've had, now that I've met you. Visandra, you are entirely too charming and clever to be alone so long."

"I could say the same for you," she replied in a soft, sincere tone.

"Oh, no, I wasn't alone," he said with a light laugh. "I've had my share of loves and losses, and a marriage once before. She died too young."

"What?"

The word was flat. No surprise, no anger. It barely revealed her confusion.

"It didn't seem worth mentioning. There were no children."

"I'm sorry for your loss," I mumbled quickly. They were the only words I could think to say without coming between the two of them. They were a rote response I'd heard from

139

others so many times when Agrad said he was an orphan.

It stopped them both. Drav flashed me a grateful, if tight-lipped, smile. Visandra took a moment to turn and look at me, but there was a touch of disappointment in her frustration. Her face was erased of emotion in an instant before she turned on Drav again.

"If I die," she said, "will you be so flippant about it?"

"It was a long time ago."

"How long ago could it have been?"

That's the point when I decided I should leave.

"Well, a few centuries..."

A decision, however, is not an action.

"Centuries? I thought you were human."

"Decades. I meant decades!"

I should have left.

"No. You didn't. What are you if you're not human?"

But there was no way I was leaving now.

"Why does it matter?"

"You look human," Visandra said. "Your ears are round like a human, not pointed like an elf. You're not overly tall, or overly short. If you're under a spell, I want to know what my children will be before I bear them." Now her words were downright chill. "If I'd been given the chance to marry Ysili instead, I'd know that he's only half human, and that our children might have his blue hair, or be a bit too pale, but I wouldn't be surprised by a sudden dwarf, or elf, or hobgoblin, or something else entirely."

"To be fair," I said, "I really don't know what a water spirit's lineage would bring, other than—"

"Shut up, Ysili," Visandra whirled on me. "Just shut up. Unless you're offering me an alternative, I don't want to hear another word from you tonight."

Again I thought, I should have left earlier.

And I should have kept quiet in that moment.

I didn't, of course.

Doing what I was supposed to do was never a strong point of mine. "You never told me I was a viable alternative. You never even hinted that you were remotely interested in me. The only time it came up was when you apologized for your father's comment when we met."

"You only ever talked about Agrad! You wrote entire letters to me about how pretty he was, and how you wished he was a girl, or how it wouldn't even matter if he would just look at you the same way!"

Something in me shut down. Numbly, I pushed my chair back and stood. "I'm not interested in him anymore, not that it matters."

"So, you're admitting that you're interested in my betrothed?" Drav lifted an eyebrow archly.

"No, that's not–" I cut myself off with a shake of my head, frustrated. "She's been my only real friend for years. The only person I could be myself around, the only person I could talk to, honestly." I felt so incredibly awkward, standing there, trying not to hurt Visandra and not knowing which direction to go with the conversation to make sure of it. "I'm not admitting anything other than my life is pretty terrible right now, and watching the two of you fight when all I want for Visandra is happiness is not helping that feeling at all."

That's when I realized how quiet the dining hall had become. Yes, a lot had emptied out over the course of the meal, but that wasn't entirely the source of the silence. I'd been so wrapped up in the argument that I'd missed the whispers and glances from those who were still present.

I looked around, then straightened my vest and took a step back. "I don't care what you choose, or who you decide to spend your life with. Go and be a hermit, if it would make you happy, just let me know you'll still make me a part of your life. I still need my friend."

"Then I wouldn't be a hermit, would I?" She was suppressing a laugh, and I took that as a good sign.

"No, I suppose not." I tried a smile in return. It was a bit forced, but real.

It fell entirely when Drav put a hand over Visandra's.

"You won't get rid of me that easily," he said, voice soft and seemingly kind, but I thought there was an undercurrent of danger, of possession to his tone.

"I never said I wanted to be rid of you," she hurried to reply. "Either of you. I'm not going to be a hermit, that was Ysili's idea, not mine."

"Calm down," Drav said. "It was a joke."

The room around us was still as quiet as if we were performers on a stage. If the whole palace didn't know every word of this conversation as it happened, they would by morning.

Maybe I should have been embarrassed.

"Are you going to allow her to have friends, once you own her? That's how arranged marriage works, isn't it? It's a passing of possessions, buying and selling women as brides to bear a child."

That broke the silence in the room, eliciting gasps that finally made Drav and Visandra realize how intently they were being watched.

"It's why I didn't like your father's insinuations," I added.

"I've been passed around like an unwanted possession. I won't be party to it."

The two of them didn't so much as glance at each other.

"You didn't step up to save me from such a fate."

"I'm not buying her!"

They both spoke at the same time, eyes going from me to the room around us.

I shook my head. "Drav, you don't even know her. You only know that she'd give you attractive children."

"What would you have me do, Ysili?" Visandra was going quiet, but intense. "Be alone the rest of my life while I wait for someone who doesn't want me?"

"Marry me," I said. "Tell your father to go jump in a lake and be with me if you want to. I don't have much to offer but my worthless name, not yet, but I'll work twice as hard as anyone to give you the life you deserve."

Drav didn't protest.

He sat still in his chair, a look of faint amusement crossed his countenance, but he kept his silence.

Visandra looked at me, then him, then me again.

"Are you serious? You're asking me NOW?"

"I'm an idiot," I said, "but not enough of an idiot to just watch you walk away if there's even a small chance I won't end up dead and alone with nothing to show but regrets."

She stared at me, eyes wide and sort of bugged out, and then she looked at Drav.

He shrugged.

The bastard simply shrugged.

"You'd just let me walk away?" she accused him.

"I'm nothing if not patient," Drav said. "Go and marry your childhood crush. I'll still be here when he's gone. What's a few years, this way or that?"

Visandra moved to slap him across the face, but he grabbed her wrist and started to laugh.

"I won't leave you," I swore, unsettled by the insinuation in Drav's tone.

Drav laughed harder, then stood and left the dining hall.

Visandra balled her hands into fists and looked like she wanted to chase after him. Not to change his mind, but to make another attempt at striking him.

Instead she turned to me.

"You'd better not leave me," she said, storm clouds in her eyes. "If you do, I'll make your privates public by nailing them to a door."

I winced, believing her authenticity and her ire.

"You don't need to resort to threats," I said. "I swear, I'm yours until the day I die."

IX - The Happy Ending

The next day was interesting, to say the least. First thing in the morning I was summoned to a formal audience with Lord Ceolwyn for the first time since we'd returned to Anogrin. Oh, we'd run into each other in the halls on occasion, we'd spoken (tersely on my part) in social situations, but a formal summons hadn't happened since I'd lit the table in the great hall on fire as a child.

"Take a seat," he said, stern and authoritative as he always was in his office.

I bowed first, of course, as protocol required. It was funny to me, how automatically I performed gestures of respect I'd learned as a child, though I hadn't had a reason in so many years.

Funny, just like how I couldn't bring myself to speak until invited to, while sitting in this room.

"Word has reached me that you are responsible for a disruption to the evening meal last night. Is this true?"

"No, Lord Ceolwyn."

"No?" His lips curled in a weary smile. "You didn't spring up on your feet, insult a diplomat from Lorwyn, and propose marriage to a woman the diplomat is engaged to?"

"They started it," I said, but it sounded so ridiculously childish that I coughed to clear my throat and started again. "It's a bit more complicated than that, My Lord, but I did all of those things for—"

"Yes," he interrupted me, "I'm sure you had your reasons. Mistress Cerine was your point of contact on the way to Cairnborough, yes?"

"She's been my friend for years," I added. "She was the only person I could be myself around."

Lord Ceolwyn nodded and drummed his fingers on the arm of his chair, taking a few moments to think. "I'm not too familiar with Drav Anates, he's been elsewhere, but if he raises a protest—"

"He won't!"

Lord Krecek Ceolwyn, wizard of the country of Ceolwyn, equal to a god in magic potential, former High Priest of the Goddess of Magic, stared at me with both eyebrows raised and an ever-so-slight frown that sent a shiver down my spine. I felt his displeasure at being interrupted on a visceral level, twisting my guts and making my heart skip a beat in a moment of terror. It was a shadow of what Agrad had wrought, but all the worse for the needle-like focus he bore upon me.

"He said he wouldn't." I forced the words out in a voice that threatened to be reminiscent of an adolescent squeak.

Lord Ceolwyn nodded thoughtfully. "Drav still might," he said. "It would be his right, no matter what he said in the moment." He drummed his fingers on the chair again, then leaned forward. "I'll set that aside for now and deal with it if or when Modarian brings it up. Thankfully we're fairly friendly. This brings me to the crux of the matter, however. Your position within these walls."

My heart sank. This was the point that I would finally be turned out on my own and abandoned completely. I'd have nothing to offer Visandra, and she would be stuck with a pauper or forced to return to Drav. A veritable chasm had opened before me, and I prepared myself to be pushed in.

But then I stopped myself. I had all these thoughts as if I hadn't just weeks ago been contemplating an informal departure of my own. Even if I lost everything, I could start again. Maybe she'd be happy at a chance to start anew. Or, perhaps she'd leave me, and I'd find someone else. Someone nearly as pretty. Someone nearly as fun and exciting.

It wouldn't be ideal, but it wasn't the end of me.

"I'd like to talk about that, too," I said. "Before you say anything, please hear me out. Lord Ceolwyn, I've been giving this a lot of thought, and I would have asked this sooner or later. Being aimless doesn't suit me. I'd like to formally petition to join the guard."

"You'd like to be a member of my guard?" He looked surprised, and a touch confused. He then laughed. "I expected you to demand your freedom, or to be sent elsewhere for further education. I wouldn't have expected you to have any desire to protect me."

"No, My Lord." It took real effort not to smirk. "I'd like to protect innocent people who get near enough to you to suffer under the cloud of bad luck that surrounds you." I was challenging him by throwing out a truth no one else dared say to his face. I hadn't been able to shoot him with an arrow, but this was a weapon I knew I could aim true.

His face went still the way only an elf's could. Not like stone, but like a tree; alive but moved only peripherally by the wind. He breathed, his wispy hair stirred, but only barely.

Lord Ceolwyn was silent, but I was patient. I'd said the words I'd wanted to say. I was ready to wait the rest of my life for an answer, to see if he would accept my terms.

"You've already been training with Reyen," he said. "Clearly he sees some potential in you, to have told you so much already."

"Yes, my Lord."

"If I denied your petition, what would you do with your life?"

My mouth went dry. My anxiety rose again, telling me that I'd spoken my heart to Visandra for nothing, that my bluff had been called, that I had no hope and no future and I was as worthless as I'd always been afraid I was and I was about to be cast aside by Krecek as I'd been cast aside by my parents and by Agrad and what else could I even have expected —

"I don't know." I clenched my hands together in my lap and stared at them. "I'd gather my belongings and leave. I wouldn't burden you with my presence ever again."

147

He let out a long sigh, and I caught something reminiscent of sadness shadow his eyes. "Very well, I accept your service." He smiled at me, placid as a small lake on a still day. "This will make it easier to handle any protest from Lorwyn, if you've sworn your loyalty and service to me. Your motivations can be your own, of course. Every member of my guard has their reasons for why they've joined. I demand unwavering obedience no matter your motive, and your absolute loyalty no matter what I ask of you."

"I've already sworn I'd stay by Visandra's side. I can't break that."

He surprised me with a gentle smile. "For the price of your loyalty to me, I'll see to it that you can fulfill your vow to her. She, at least, is an innocent in this matter. I'll even formalize your union myself, should the two of you desire."

"I'll ask her," I said. "I'm sure she will be honored."

She probably would, too. It was possibly the best wedding gift I could give her.

But I'd be trapped. I'd never be free.

Visandra is worth it, I thought to myself.

"I'm sure she will," he agreed. "What of you?"

She was worth selling my freedom for her happiness.

"I'd be honored as well, Lord Ceolwyn. Thank you."

I found Visandra saying a farewell to Drav in the courtyard. When I saw tears in her eyes I was nearly moved to rage, but I had to be on my best behavior now. I had responsibilities now, and loyalty to someone who could erase me with a casual gesture. Instead I held my silence and stood back until Drav waved me over to join them.

"I'm patient," he said to her, part of what they'd been saying before I joined them. "I can afford to be." Drav then smiled at me. "The better man won. Shouldn't you be overjoyed?"

"I am. I swear I am." My voice betrayed me, though. "I just escaped a formal summons over the ruckus the two of you caused last night."

Drav had the decency to wince in sympathy. "Because I'm an ambassador?"

I nodded.

Visandra frowned. "I thought the rumors wouldn't spread that far that fast. I meant to have it all straightened out before he heard a word about it."

"You weren't punished over it, were you?" An unusual swirl of magic surrounded Drav for a moment.

How should I answer that? "He accepted my request to be a member of the guard. He offered to officiate the wedding himself."

"Not much of a punishment, then." The magic was gone, whatever it had been. Drav mounted his horse and nodded down at me. "Be good to her. Or else."

"You're threatening me?" I tried to laugh, but it caught in my throat.

I never joke when it comes to revenge. Be good to her or else.

I don't know why the words popped into my head. Out loud I'd only heard the word "yes" before Drav rode away.

Visandra was wiping away more tears, but she was smiling. "Lord Ceolwyn really offered to officiate our wedding? You said yes, right? Tell me you said yes."

149

"Of course I said yes." I hugged her tight.

She was as delighted as I knew she'd be, and from that point nothing else mattered. Drav and his odd magic drifted from my mind. Agrad was a footnote in my distant history. My vow to serve Krecek was only background noise to this moment. I'd made my love happy. I'd done the right thing.

Visandra was all that mattered.

The wedding was chaos. So far, the marriage has been much better, much calmer, and worth everything. It took us a year and a half, and a little help, for Visandra to find herself with child. I might have been able to get that help from Lord Ceolwyn, but I didn't want a child who could only exist by the whim and will of a wizard. Instead, we only needed a small amount of help of a mage and a healer Visandra had befriended. It was a small victory for her, but it meant the world to me.

The day Chalaine came into my life I stopped wishing for freedom. If I was chained to her and her mother, so be it. My darling daughter has been the world to me. She's also been the greatest terror I've ever faced. The way I've grown up, the way I've been discarded and used, I was afraid I'd do the same.

I'm sure I haven't been the perfect parent. What I have done is be the best parent I could be.

As I write this, we're expecting Arment, named after Visandra's father. Chalaine is excited to have a brother some days. Other days, she's too wrapped up in whatever is going on with her friends to remember that our family is about to get bigger.

...and Lord Ceolwyn has brought Agrad to the palace.

I saw him and my heart skipped a beat. I'm still conflicted. I wanted to rush to his side and give him a hug and tell him how excited I was to see him again. I wanted to bring him home with me, introduce him to Chalaine and tell him about Visandra.

He looked through me as if we'd never met before.

I remembered the fear and hopelessness of the last time I'd seen him.

I'm glad he left.

My life has been better without him.

Longing is easily replaced with anger, I suppose.

I have my family, and I don't need him.

Final Interlude

Visandra pulled the pages from the box she'd put Ysili's most treasured possessions in after his death. She ran her fingers over the first page. "It's funny how the biggest changes in life come in sudden moments..." she whispered to herself, reading the opening words as if saying them would bring a part of her first husband back.

"This is what he wrote?"

She looked at Lord Verwyn and clutched the pages to her chest a moment, protective. "You won't like everything he said. He never expected you to know this existed, I think he wrote it all just to sort out his feelings. At first he didn't even want me to read any of it."

"I understand." Verwyn held out a hand though, and she found herself handing the stack over to him. "Please, think of me as Agrad. Ysili did. I have no need of titles, especially for someone who helped me when I needed it."

"Help you?" Visandra's laugh was as bitter as a lemon peel. "It wasn't out of kindness. I was ordered, like Ysili was. Put that in your mind before you start reading."

Agrad nodded.

He didn't turn the pages. His fingers hovered over them, and that was all. Agrad handed it all back, and there was a faint whiff of dust and vanilla in the air.

"I'm sorry for inconveniencing you," he said. "I needed to know, to set my mind at rest."

"You could have had him," she whispered, unsure why the words came to her mouth at all. "If you'd asked Ysili at any point, ever, he'd have dropped everything for you. Even me."

"No." Agrad placed a hand on her arm, and warm comfort settled over her. "He chose you. He died devoted to you and loathing me, as it should be." A sad smile touched his lips, his eyes, and he shook his head. "I'm glad he found someone who could be better for him than I ever was. If you or your children ever need anything from me, I'll protect you to the end."

"Even if I had children with Drav?" She'd remarried, of course, and Drav had only offered her comfort and patience. Somehow he'd known that Ysili's days were limited, and had been gracious enough to give her time so she could love them

152

both.

Agrad nodded. "I don't think any child of his would need protection, but yes. If they do, I will."

"What do you mean?"

The wizard hesitated. "You don't know? He hasn't told you?"

"What?"

"It's none of my business to tell you. I've overstayed my welcome."

Agrad vanished.

And Visandra forgot he'd been there.

Dawnsday

There were two traditional holidays that were celebrated by staying awake to greet the dawn. Nightwatch, where everyone gathered together in love and support, giving gifts and lighting fires to bring light back into the world; and Dawnsday to celebrate the light and revel in all the gifts that summer would bring. It was a celebration of fertility, and a time to abandon oneself in the simple pleasures of being alive.

Agrad preferred Nightwatch to Dawnsday, despite the cold. He always had, and he suspected he always would. Nightwatch was for family and closeness and creating your own warmth and love. Dawnsday was loud and boisterous and sometimes a bit frightening with all of the costumes and fire dancers and drinking and revelry that often separated families into the different sorts of fun they'd prefer to indulge in. His last Dawnsday in Cairnborough he had stumbled upon more than one orgy, and at last he understood why he'd felt so left out of the holiday as a child.

This Dawnsday was different, though. The palace in Verwyn was somewhat isolated, and he'd willingly dismissed all who lived or worked there to join in the revelry.

"Will you be joining in, Master Verwyn?"

Agrad looked at Byrek in surprise, wondering if it was an invitation or a reminder of some sort of duty he should have known. "I hadn't planned on it," he replied slowly.

Byrek shook his head and simply left, leaving Agrad with a knot in his stomach over the implied disapproval. Agrad chewed on his lower lip, but he wanted nothing to do with

154

loud celebrations right now. He was the wizard here. He would celebrate the way he wanted.

Squaring his shoulders, Agrad grabbed a blanket and a pillow, and he simply walked away. He technically wasn't supposed to leave the palace grounds without letting Byrek know first, but it was a holiday, and he was sure that it wouldn't matter as long as he returned.

The clearing was one he'd found a few weeks before, with a flat marble bolder in the center that made him think of ancient altars to the gods. Had it been used as one, in prehistoric times? What sort of offerings would have been left there, if it had? He felt Nalia stir in the back of his mind as if his speculation touched her in some way, so he turned his thoughts to other things as he draped the blanket across the stone surface and sat upon it.

Must you always profane what once was sacred?

The voice of the goddess was tired, resigned. Apparently trying to shift his thoughts to first stage alchemical transmutations hadn't been enough to quell her. Agrad didn't know yet how to shut her out and ignore her, now that she had awakened. Really, on some of his lonelier days, he wasn't entirely sure he wanted to silence her. No one else in the palace had said more than a handful of words to him since the disaster of a first day.

"How should I know what's sacred and what's not?" It was dangerous to talk to her, to acknowledge her at all, but he did it anyway this time. Some part of her sounded as lonely as he was, and he couldn't ignore that, no matter what others warned him.

You knew. The feeling you have here that lead to your speculation. You're no longer a child of idle imagination.

155

"It was just a feeling," Agrad said, laying down upon the stone and staring at the sky. Sunset colors were fading to black, and stars were beginning to shine. "Besides, I'm a wizard. Isn't that the greatest profanity ever?"

You're an elemental, she corrected gently. *The wizard who killed me is dead.*

"My power is still stolen," he said, shifting uncomfortably. "And I know you hate me for it. You'd kill me, if you ever got free.

I'd kill you by getting free. So, if I were to get free, it wouldn't be possible for me to kill you.

"Oh, that's a comfort," he said crossly. "So, you really were trying to kill me a couple months ago? Back in Cairnfeld?"

Of course.

Anger stabbed through him, and he glared up at nothing. "I'm glad you're dead," he muttered. "If you weren't, I think I'd have to kill you myself just for that."

Uneasy silence followed for a great portion of the night, as they mulled over their mutual resentments. For his part, Agrad had to admit to himself that he wasn't really glad that the goddess was dead. He didn't know what to feel about her current state at all, really. He'd just wanted to hurt her, for being so indifferent about the possibility of his death. It was a bit surprising to him that his heated response had actually had the intended result.

I've driven every Verwyn wizard from Davri onward to death. I was Nalia, goddess of magic! The wizards were MINE! You've betrayed me. Every single one of you. Of course I want you dead!

Her silent tirade startled him from his thoughts of making peace or offering a truce of some sort. He'd actually jumped, sitting up and holding his hand over his rapidly beating heart from surprise, since she'd been silent for so long.

"Okay," he gasped, pulling his pillow to his chest. "I get the picture. You hate us. And I'm stuck with you. Great. But, it's not getting YOU anywhere, either. Take all the vengeance you want, over and over, but the first Verwyn is the one who killed you. Not me, and not any of the rest of us."

He could feel the chaos of her thoughts, but couldn't put meaning to any of them. It seemed like a pure explosion of anger and helplessness and indignation, but there were other emotions roiling in the mixture that he couldn't begin to identify.

And, finally, she somehow set it all aside. *You could be right, but it doesn't matter. Vengeance and hatred aren't logical, and my hatred is without end. I'll still kill you, if I have the chance.*

"I'll just try not to give you the chance," he sighed. What else could he say? "I don't want to die."

I didn't, either.

"Well, there's something we can agree on. Dying is bad. Truce?"

No, but nice try.

He hadn't expected it to work, but the mood was lighter now and that was what he had really wanted. "You'll come around some day. Mark my words." He laughed, lying down again to stare up at the stars.

Never, she thought, but there was a smile implied in her tone. She could be soft, and she could be kind. If the situation had been different....

"I know better, though," he said in reply to the unvoiced feeling they'd shared. "If things were different, I'd have simply grown up fearing gods and not wizards. You can't plant such suggestions in my head."

157

You'd still be powerful. The time of gods could have seen you as a high priest, easily. You could have known my approval and not my approbation.

"Maybe. But, now we'll never know," he said, and a fallen star streaked across the sky. "But if you think I could have, perhaps it is your mind you should be trying to change. Not mine. The rest of my life can be hell for you, or for both of us. But, perhaps, it doesn't need to be."

She fell silent again, and this time even her powerful emotions were self-contained. The rest of the night they spent as isolated from each other as they could be, until the dawn.

"Blessed Dawnsday, merry reveler," Agrad remembered the old invocation. "May the year ahead be filled with abundance and growth."

Blessed Dawnsday, Nalia whispered within his mind.

Unsaid

"When you were Davri," Krecek began softly, sitting across from Agrad with centuries of history haunting his eyes.

Agrad waited, smiling sadly. "What?"

"Nothing," Krecek said. "It's morbid of me to even ask."

Agrad set down his cup, gazing at Krecek with those innocent yet maddeningly enigmatic eyes of his. "I can think of so many things you might want to ask of Davri. Morbid or not, ask me."

Krecek maintained his silence with a shake of his head.

"Did you want to ask me what it's like to die? Now that Baedrogan is dead, what sort of afterlife is there? Nalia alone could answer those. Let's see. Dying hurts, mostly, until the spirit and the body agree to part ways. At that point it's peaceful. Baedrogan in his wisdom, knowing he would die, had already set up a system where our spirits would have a peaceful place to rest. The one exception he made was for us. Wizards and gods. We do not rest, we return. He did that to us, and I don't know if it was a punishment or a boon, but that's what he did."

"I figured that much out myself," Krecek said, looking briefly irritated. "It's just something I've thought of, off and on, since Davri died."

Agrad waited silently.

"Davri had visions. Do you remember them?"

"That's not morbid," Agrad said, chuckling slightly and shaking his head. "Yes. I remember them all. From the very first time he knew war was coming, to the very last vision he

159

had of me as he died. Some came to pass. Others, thankfully, did not. The memories of the visions are all here in my mind."

Krecek took a deep breath. "He knew. Davri knew he was going to die ahead of time. I put it together from things he said before it happened. But--did he choose to die?"

Agrad inhaled sharply, eyes wide and, for a moment, afraid. The play of emotion that crossed his face was fascinating as well as telling. "That's a very, very difficult question to answer," he said, voice cracking on the first very. "You have to understand, it wasn't easy for him. There was so much to live for. So much, in fact, that he rushed toward his fate because he was terrified he wouldn't be able to do it if he had stopped to think about it too much."

"So, it was a choice," Krecek said, frowning. "It was, essentially, suicide."

"Don't think of it like that." Agrad stood, only to walk around the table and kneel next to Krecek. "If you think of it like suicide, then you'll start to think it could have been stopped. That you could have saved me, if you'd just tried hard enough. That I left you behind when you needed me most. I hated that I had to make that choice. I wish I could have hidden in Byrek's arms forever, doing my best to pretend I wasn't the only one who could do what needed to be done."

"It's hard not to take it personally when we'd--I mean, it had only been a week before, that we..." Krecek stumbled over his words. "Gods...that is not what I meant to say."

"Davri was...torn on that part. If it helps any." He took Krecek's hands and looked into his eyes. "He didn't mean to hurt you. He was just so lonely, and terrified, and he knew you felt the same. He knew it would hurt Nalia, too. They

160

hated each other so much..." Agrad let go to put his own hands to his temples, as if the thought of how much they hated each other, and having them both within, was a cause of pain.

"I thought you'd made peace," Krecek said gently, placing a hand on Agrad's cheek.

"Peace, yes, but the pain is still there from both of them," Agrad said. "They both loved you, in their own ways, and were jealous of each other. Being a wizard was sheer hell for both of them." Agrad's eyes lost focus, and the air vibrated with a tingle of magic not many would be able to feel. It used to set Krecek on edge, but now he knew it was just because he was so attuned to Nalia's presence, and the heightened power of her direct attention.

"Don't think about that time," Krecek said gently, sliding his hand to the back of Agrad's neck and pulling him closer. "It was hell for all of us, but it's in the past."

Agrad nodded and let himself be guided closer, kissing Krecek ever so gently before sitting back on his heels. "It's so hard, sometimes. I feel what Nalia felt, and the completely alien way she loved you. I feel what Davri felt, and the way he burned for Byrck but he almost pined for you with his distant admiration. And then..."

"And then?" Krecek smiled wistfully. "What do you feel, Agrad? Just you, without the two of them?"

"What I feel for you is so much different," he said. "You're the first person, the only person, I've ever been in love with. I hate myself for it, but I love you. I need you more than I've ever needed anyone. I want you in ways that make me blush to think of. I wish I could just hate you, but I know you too well now not to forgive you, for everything."

"Is that so?" Krecek's heart was beating as if it were a bird about to take flight. As if wings pressed against the inside of his chest and sought to burst forth. "You're free to hate me, you know. I know myself better than you. There's too much to ever forgive."

"Oh, I hate you," Agrad said softly. "There's plenty of it to go around. I simply love you more tha--"

"My Lord?"

Krecek looked up, startled. "I was deep in thought. Repeat yourself."

The maid gestured to his plate. "Are you finished, Lord Ceolwyn? Shall I clear your plate?"

Barely a thing had been touched, but that was hardly unusual. "Yes. My complements to the cook, and all of that." He shooed her away.

Agrad was watching him across the table. "No one has interrupted us, and you still haven't eaten?"

"I'm just tired from my journey," Krecek said. Distracted by his fantasy had been more like it, but it wasn't something he could admit. Not to the subject of his fantasy, at least. "I'll eat tomorrow. I promise."

"If you're that tired," Agrad said. He looked concerned, but he waved Krecek off. "It's fine. Go rest."

Krecek left without another word, afraid that if he lingered he would say the things he'd dreamed of saying.

Author's Note

Just so everyone knows, I had every intention of putting out my next book at LEAST a year sooner than this. I feel this needs to be front and center here, along with an apology and many thanks for all the patience everyone has shown me.

And by apology, I mean to say that my last book came out in 2020, and everything went to complete shit after that. Family deaths, friends' deaths, pet deaths, my first ride in an ambulance, my first stay at a hospital where I didn't come home as or with a brand-new human being, etc. Oh, and that "etc." is covering a lot of ground. Like I said, it was 2020 and everything went to complete shit for a while. Nobody needs details. We were all there, or you're sitting safely sometime in a future I can't imagine, and you'll know what I mean because it's in a history book you didn't want to read. There will be no sordid details from me shared in an autobiography. If you want the full story you're going to have to provide the drinks at a convention someday.

Instead of whining needlessly about something that affected everyone, I just want to thank you for reading, for having my back, and for being patient while the world fell apart for a while. And now, to writing a little bit about what I've written. All the short stories in this collection started out as writing exercises as I worked on the series. Most have been posted in Patreon as a monthly reward to my patrons, but not all.

I've kept the stories in loosely chronological order, and I haven't included any spoilers for anything that happens after *Abomination*. There's a good chance I'll have to bookend the series with another novella and short stories/deleted scenes after book six is published. There's a story I'm working on that takes place a few centuries after the books are done and over with, but I haven't been able to share it with anyone at all yet. I'm looking forward to the day that I can!

We Are as Dreams was written on Mother's Day a few years back, exploring Nalia, her complicated ideas of motherhood, and how she viewed the subject. Thinking of motherhood from the perspective of a being who had no mother was a fun exercise and helped me delve into her motivations and personality a bit deeper.

When I wrote *Far From Home* I had just introduced Meran in *Graves of the Gods* and absolutely fell in love with him. Going further into what it means to be an elf in Kayan started the ball rolling, but it left me with a much deeper understanding of Krecek's feelings and motivations as a whole. It was a story I savored the experience of writing.

Prelude is a deleted scene from *The Arcane War*. I love the interplay between Agruet and Baedrogan, always, and wanted to make that scene a prologue, but it bogged down the beginning and I couldn't seem to make it fit anywhere else. It was heartbreaking to delete, so I'm glad I found somewhere else to share it.

Smoke and Mirrors comes from an urge I had when I thought about writing Elemental from a third person POV. In the end I kept it first person, but the chance to tell Torba and Fadal's story was irresistible. I adore Agrad's parents and the love they shared, even if it didn't end well.

Another thing I found irresistible was the chance to see Shaelek's childhood in *From Darkness*. Modarian as a wise mentor for this adorable yet haunted little girl was delightful.

Playing with how Modarian and Shaelek are different from, but similar to Agruet and Baedrogan makes me entirely too happy.

Dawnsday was the first short story/writing exercise I wrote for this universe. I'd barely written the first half of *Elemental* when I decided to play around with writing Agrad from an outside POV. In the original iteration of the story I have Agrad teleporting around different places, showing off his skills and acting out a bit more, but the point was to show how Nalia might soften to him eventually, and the peace between them felt good.

When it came to *Unsaid*, it was something I wrote before I'd finished *Elemental*, again. We all have those moments when we daydream what we want to say to someone, but can't. Exploring Krecek's vulnerability and hopelessness about Agrad brought me to a dinner that never was, and ultimately I didn't go further than this until *Abomination* when I knew how things would wind up in the end.

The heart of this collection, of course, is *Still Waters*. It began with this idea that there was so much more to Ysili than Agrad knew, which meant I couldn't put it all into *Elemental* as I wrote it. I started writing Ysili's story to keep track of why he acted certain ways, what his motivations were, and what secrets he had to keep from Agrad through the course of their friendship. He couldn't even explain himself at the end, because Yda had corrupted him by that point, so I had to tell his story separately. Thanks to the contributions of my patrons over at Patreon, I finished the tale. Reaching the end helped me deal with my own grief enough to enjoy writing again. The story ends with Ysili's death, but it's not THE end. It's an end. Just like every other story.

I'd like to conclude with my everlasting thanks to all my friends and family who made it possible for me write all this in the first place. For Josh Stomberg and his family for the gorgeous cover art you keep creating for me. For so many entertainers on YouTube who made content during the pandemic that distracted me, or forced me to deal with my emotions. (Memento Mori, my friends.) And most of all, for my patrons on Patreon who have kept believing in me. Especially Amy Lauritzen, Em Ascano, Kimberlie Gardner, and Sabrina Zirakzadeh for your generous contributions over the years. You all rock!

About the Author

Tam Chronin is a figment of the imagination, which might be why she lives there often enough to find her main characters and convince them to share their stories.

Before becoming an author she slayed trolls for many years in the wilds of the internet. She was occasionally granted the legendary weapon, Ban Hammer, to aid in this quest. It was a relief to retire from such harrowing adventures, but for a coin and a stiff drink she might recount them over a campfire.

She lives in Phoenix, Arizona, with her family, two parakeets, three cats, a bunny, a varying number of both fish and chickens, and a vicious attack tortoise who guards the back yard.

Also By Tam Chronin

The Godslayer Series

Elemental
The Arcane War
Abomination

Still Waters and Other Tales

Upcoming:
Graves of the Gods
The Madness of Verwyn

The Graceful Death Series

Everyone Dies Alone

Upcoming:
Zombies Half Price

Made in the USA
Columbia, SC
12 February 2025